Friendship Mysteries

HEMLOCK LAKE

Mary Keane Jackson

I0769993

Copyright © 2024 Turtle Lane Publishing
All rights reserved

The characters and events portrayed in this book are fictitious.
Any similarity to real persons, living or dead, is coincidental
and not intended by the author.

No part of this book may be reproduced, or stored in a retrieval
system, or transmitted in any form or by any means, electronic,
mechanical, photocopying, recording, or otherwise, without
express written permission of the publisher.

ISBN-13: 9798990839007

Cover design by: Canva AI
Printed in the United States of America

Gentle Mother,
Peaceful Dove

Prologue

It seems like yesterday, my best friend and I were running around town, searching for clues, keeping busy until the inevitable would happen. It was absolutely the best summer of my life. Sitting on the beach and watching the waves brings me some time to reflect on our friendship.

As the waves crash, I think about your smile, laughter, and, most of all, your unending need to make me happy knowing what was to come.

Beatrice

Cancer sucks. More importantly, dying sucks. It's hard to understand how some people get cancer and others don't. How is that fair? I continue to ask myself that question over and over again. Sometimes, I think maybe they're wrong, or I will beat the odds, and other times I just figure heaven must need a person like me.

Hard to imagine how heaven could possibly need a sixteen-year-old girl. A girl that hasn't even had a first date, first kiss, or pretty much first anything, but, hey, if He needs me, He needs me.

So, yeah, I am sixteen, and my name is Beatrice. I know, Beatrice, how lame is that? My friends call me Bea. If I can leave anything on this earth for future generations, it is, please, do not, for the love of all that is holy, name your future children after an old grandparent. They will not care, and your kid, with a stupid old-fashioned name, will. Trust me on this.

I live in a teeny, tiny town. There's exactly one traffic light in the center of town, and that was added only because some lady hit a cat with her car. Everyone blamed it on there not being a traffic light, instead of blaming it on the elderly lady who was driving, while not being able to see, in the rain, at night. Were they thinking the cat would still be alive if it had only used the light to cross the road? It doesn't make much sense to me.

We live in a tiny beach town that is only known for one thing, someone claims they saw a three-headed alligator in our only lake. Seems unlikely, but when other towns have cool claims to fame, you take what you can get.

I always wished I lived in San Francisco, where they have a giant bridge, or Orlando, which has Mickey Mouse, or New York City, which has Times Square, and yet we only have the honor of some guy's word that the three-headed alligator exists. No one else has ever seen a two-headed alligator around, never mind one with three heads. Some bozo even named our town based on it, Tri-Gator, Georgia. But, who am I to make fun of the name when mine is Beatrice?

Tri-Gator, Georgia is a teeny, tiny town. We have one store that sells everything in one place, from gas to groceries to clothing. It even sells souvenirs for the vast number of people who may want to stop to visit, no one ever does. Of course, all the souvenirs are images of three-headed alligators on either mugs, T-shirts, or magnets. I would be surprised if they ever sold even one. We have one restaurant, one church, one park, one lake, and one school for every grade from first grade through high school. I have heard of other places that have separate schools for different age groups. That seems weird.

Here, you can walk from one end of the town to the other without even breaking a sweat, and yet no one, other than that one guy, has ever seen the alligator.

A few things you should know about me. First, I am addicted to true crime shows. I think I can do way better at solving crimes than the detectives they have on television. If I were going to live a long life, I would be a detective and solve crimes. I know I would rock it.

Second, my very best friend is Chloe. Lucky her, she gets a cool name and doesn't have a cancer diagnosis. But, if there's anyone I would want to stay alive, it would be her. We are the bestest of friends. We actually refer to ourselves as 'besties for the resties.' We have been calling ourselves that for as long as I can remember.

We even have matching bracelets that prove we are besties. We made them for each other when we were in summer camp in the fourth grade. Neither one of us has ever taken them off. Well, not on purpose anyway. Mine is blue and has a letter C on it for Chloe. Chloe's is green and has the letter B on it. I would feel lost without having mine. I am positive Chloe would be, too.

People say we look alike, but I don't think that's true. She has blonde hair, super blonde, whereas mine is a darker blonde. Well, that was when I had hair, of course. Cancer took that away rather quickly. She has blue eyes, *and I have brown. We are about the same height, not too tall, not too short. Since I have lost weight from the cancer, I am pretty thin, and she is more normal-looking. In my heart, we are identical, but in reality, not so much. They probably just think that because we are always together.*

Third, I don't have long to live. I heard the doctors say the word hospice. I had no idea what it was, so I researched the word in our encyclopedia. We have every book in the series except for the letter G. No one seems to know what happened to the G book. I think someone had to do a book report on Georgia and just never put it back.

The word hospice says a person has six months left to live. It seems weird that they will know that, but I do appreciate science, so I'm not questioning it. I mean, if a million scientists came up with it, enough to have it documented in the encyclopedia, then who am I to disagree?

Lastly, Tommy is the cutest boy in the tenth grade, although he does not know that I exist, yet.

So, I decided to leave a few things for when I am, you know, gone. One is a list for my mom of things she can and cannot do after I'm gone. This list cannot be opened until I have moved on. I wrote it and left it with Chloe with explicit instructions on when my mom could have it. No one even knows it exists, except us two.

Chloe pinky promised she wouldn't read it until the time comes. She put it in her special edition, super safe, pink Barbie locker. Of course, pretty much every teenage girl in the world has the same one, all with identical keys, but it still feels super safe.

The other thing is, I'm going to document my last summer with Chloe. Not much exciting usually happens, but we are calling it the 'Summer of C.' Meaning Summer of Cancer. Let's hope some fun things happen, so I have some fun stuff to write about.

Chloe

I am Chloe. Bea asked me to add to her special book with a few words, so let's see. Bea is my best friend of all time. Besties for the resties. We met when we were super little. My mom says we met when we were both in diapers. Not sure if that's true, but it feels like it could be.

We moved in next door to Bea when I just turned one. Bea means the world to me. I can tell her anything, and I know she has my back.

We even have a special code word to prove it. The word marshmallow is our special word. Anytime we feel like we need a hug or need to tell each other that we have each other's back, our go-to word is marshmallow. We were young when we came up with it. It was one time we were sleeping over at Bea's house. Bea thought she heard something under the bed and instead of yelling 'monster', she yelled 'marshmallow'. We were laughing so hard that the monster didn't seem so scary. Since then, anytime we feel scared, alone, or need extra love, we say marshmallow. We usually either grab each other's hand or a quick hug and instantly feel better.

I would do anything for Bea. Well, except die. I probably wouldn't do that. That would seem stupid. I don't think it would save her, and I'm super afraid of bugs. I couldn't handle being buried in a hole. I told Bea that, and she said she feared bugs too, but she has a plan. Not exactly sure what that means, but if Bea says she's on to something, then she must be all set.

When Bea told me she had the big C word, I cried for a week straight. I still get upset when I think about it. But I know when she leaves, she will come and find me. She promised.

One way or another, Bea will always be with me. Although, if she does crazy stuff to scare me just because she can, I will not be thrilled.

We plan to spend every single day together this summer. I mean every second. The only rule we have is we can't talk about the C word, not at all. We must pretend it isn't a thing. I'm all for it. Maybe if we don't mention it, it'll go away.

We pinky promised we would be with each other all the time. We'll sleep at each other's house and never be apart. We're going to cram in as much as we can before she leaves. We are super ready for the 'Summer of C'. It officially starts bright and early tomorrow morning.

7:00 AM we meet at the big rock between our houses.

Beatrice

I should have said 8:00 AM. I'm so sleepy, and it feels so cold out here. How's that even possible when it's eighty-two degrees already? Probably has to do with me having like four strands of hair.

Lucky for me, it's summer, and I can wear my favorite baseball hat. It's purple and has a picture of a dog on it. Too bad it didn't have a fleece lining inside to warm my shiny, bald head. Chloe had better come soon, or I will have to go look for her, and that seems like it will take too much effort. In reality, it really isn't. Her house is right next door.

From my bedroom window, I can see right into hers and hers into mine. I've heard the houses are called ranch style, not sure why, since we definitely don't live on a ranch. Our yards are kind of small.

Since we don't have a fence around them, we pretend both single yards make up one not-so-tiny yard. My house is yellow, and hers is white. I keep asking my dad to paint ours white to match Chloe's, but my dad keeps saying no.

"Hi, Bea." Finally, Chloe comes out of her house and walks toward the big rock.

"Hey, Chloe. Are we ready for the adventure to begin?"

"Of course I'm ready. Wouldn't miss it, but first I need some type of food. I'm so hungry, please tell me we can grab food?"

"Yes, please. But first, I have to go to Mr. McBean's house and walk Peanut."

Mr. McBean is really old and has a hard time even walking around inside his house, never mind trying to walk a giant dog down the street.

Mr. McBean lives right next door to me, on the left. Chloe is right next door on the right. Pretty lucky for me. Mr. McBean is the nicest man on the planet, well, except for my dad, of course. My dad wins that one, hands down. We'll get more on my dad as we go. Mr. McBean is always, and I mean always, happy to see me. Not exactly sure why, maybe because he seems a smidge lonely.

He had a wife, but she died a few years back. Since then, it sometimes seems like I'm all he has. I like to think I'm the highlight of his day. He always asks me to sit in his house or out on his deck and talk about stuff, usually about TV. He loves crime shows, too. There's one crime show we always talk about called, 'Murder in a Day'.

Each day, the show tells a crime that you need to solve based on the clues you find, and the next day, they tell you what really happened. It's supposed to be a true crime, although some stories are pretty hard to think that's the case. Each time I go over to Mr. McBean's house, we talk about what we think happened and who committed the crime.

Then, the next day, we see who was right. I have to say, I'm usually right. That's why I know I'd make a good detective. Chloe doesn't come with me all the time, but since it's the 'Summer of C,' she'll be with us from now on.

Maybe after I die, Chloe can continue spending time with Mr. McBean, that'd make me happy. I'd really feel bad if Mr. McBean had no one to talk to every day.

Mr. McBean knows I have cancer. We usually talk a little about how my treatments are going. I haven't told him yet that I won't live too much longer, that's a hard thing to say to someone.

Only a few people know the situation. I really don't want too many people to know. I told Mr. McBean that the 'Summer of C' meant crime, not cancer. I'm not sure if he believed me or not. I'd hate to have people feel bad for me. I have enough to worry about, like how it will happen and when. Like, will my heart just stop, or will I slowly get more and more tired and just not wake up one day? My doctor hasn't told me that yet.

I asked a few times, and she just said, "Try to not think about it." Yeah, like that's easy to do. I may die tomorrow and not even know it.

One thing about Mr. McBean is that he's super smart. He knows a little bit about pretty much everything we talk about. Whether it's history, science stuff, or even math. Math I'm not very good at, and I see no reason for algebra. I do not care in the least what X is, and as soon as the teacher added Y into the mix, I was even more disinterested.

We walk up to Mr. McBean's door and knock.

Mr. McBean, as always, is smiling when he opens the door and sees me standing there. Especially since I have Chloe in tow.

"Hi, Mr. McBean, hi Peanut." I can't help but to pet Peanut, since he nudged over to me and put his head in my hand.

"Well, hello, Bea and Chloe. How are you two on this fine day? It is a glorious day to be alive. The sun is out, your summer vacation has started, and the world is your oyster."

The world is my oyster? Who says that? And glorious? Nobody says that, either. Mr. McBean is also what I'd call an odd duck. Me and Chloe just roll our eyes at each other and giggle.

"What's so funny, girls? What are you two laughing about? Did I miss something?"

"Nothing," we both answer at the same time, which makes us giggle even more.

Mr. McBean offers us a soda pop, and we walk toward his back deck. Peanut's walking around the fenced-in yard smelling everything like it changed in the past few hours since he was out last.

"So, girls, yesterday's episode, what did you think?" So it begins.

I think talking about each episode is the highlight of Mr. McBean's day. He grabs his pad with his notes listed and we head to the patio table to get comfortable.

We get right to it, I start, and "I think it was the ex-husband. He seemed to be not so truthful, and all the evidence points to him. First, he was cheating on his wife, which caused the divorce, abused her, and has no alibi. What do you guys think?"

"I think it was the son. Don't forget, he's the one who was going to get all the money since his parents split up. It didn't seem like he really liked his mom either," Chloe responds.

Mr. McBean says, "I agree with Chloe. You need to follow the money. The ex-husband clearly didn't like his wife too much. But I don't see what he was going to gain from her dying. Doesn't seem like much."

"But didn't they say the son had an alibi? He was in his Biology class on campus. How could he get all the way to her house, kill her, and get back? The campus is quite far from the home, right?" I reply.

"Bea, I think you may be on to something," Mr. McBean answers.

"I don't know. My gut is still telling me it was the son," Chloe responds.

For most of the summer, this is how it went. We would talk, debate, and review it when we saw the next episode. Mr. McBean seemed to like true crime shows even more than I did. Although it turned out, I was right. It was the ex-husband, after all. It usually is.

Each day, Chloe and I would walk over to Mr. McBean's house, talk for a while, and walk Peanut. Each day was perfect. We spent each afternoon at the beach down the street. I was in heaven, at least what I'd hoped heaven would be like.

Then things started to change.

Beatrice

Six weeks into our magical school vacation, our 'Summer of C,' a few things went terribly wrong. First, we saw Tommy at the beach yesterday, and we were both in bathing suits. Oh my gosh, bathing suits. For the love of God, why did Tommy have to see us in our bikinis? Talk about being mortified.

He actually looked over at me and Chloe, smiled, waved, and ran off. There's not one girl at age sixteen who wants any boy to see them in a bathing suit, never mind the cutest boy in the school. Kill me now.

Next, my doctor called my dad yesterday to go over my latest biopsy. After suppertime, my parents sat Chloe and me down and told us that the cancer was worse. They use the word, progressed. I didn't understand all of it, but the words advanced, metastasized, and terminal were all used. All pretty bad words in a cancer diagnosis. I cried, and so did Chloe. I whispered marshmallow, and she put her arm around me. We stayed like that until I stopped crying.

My parents kept saying, "It'll be okay. We'll get through this." But how? The only way we get through this is with me dying, and everyone else gets to keep on living.

If all of that wasn't bad enough, the next morning, Chloe and I set out to go walk Peanut, and things went way off the rails.

"Okey dokey, Bea, let's get moving. I can't believe you're still going to walk Peanut. I mean, I know you love him, but wasn't it supposed to be a short-term thing? I thought after talking to your parents last night, maybe we should take the day off. I know Mr. McBean fell last week, but hasn't he healed from his fall yet? I thought he just twisted his ankle?"

I respond, "He did. And he's fine now, but I love Peanut. He's the sweetest dog ever. I don't want to stop, and I think Mr. McBean likes that I still walk Peanut for him. We never really talk about me walking Peanut, I just keep doing it. Just because of what happened last night, I don't want to stop. I think it is better to keep busy and not have time to think too much. I just show up, take Peanut, and then bring him back. Mr. McBean always says thank you. I think it just works for him. He is old, ya know."

"He must be like a million years old. Ha-ha."

"Exactly, Chloe."

We start walking to Mr. McBean's house. Mr. McBean is old, like really old, although, oddly, he still drives. Although I'm pretty sure he shouldn't. I've seen him drive over the curb near his house a ton of times. I try to stay off that curb so he doesn't run me down. I know I'm dying, but I don't want to go before I need to.

After Mr. McBean fell, he really had no one to help him. His daughter is a major jerk and doesn't want to help him. I wasn't that upset that she didn't want to help because that meant I would be needed.

Peanut is the best, and I was happy to help. He's a typical lab, super chubby, and super friendly. He's so excited when I show up. His tail doesn't stop wagging and his big butt shakes. It's hilarious. Although, some days, I have to drag myself out of bed to go get him. Good thing Peanut is so cute.

As we walk over toward his house, I stop and say,

"Hey, Chloe. That's weird. Mr. McBean's car isn't here."

"Maybe he had to run an errand. Do you have a key?"

"No. My mom does, but I never needed it. He's always home."

"Let's check the door, maybe he let one of his buddies use the car."

One thing about Chloe, she isn't afraid of anything. I know, from watching horror flicks, you never go first to a door and try to open it. Who knows what can be behind the door?

"I suppose I have to go first?" Chloe says.

"That's why we're best friends, Chloe. You know me so well."

"Ugh."

Chloe slowly walks to the door. I stay right behind her. Well, not right behind her, about six steps behind her, you know, cause of scary monster stuff.

"It doesn't look like anyone's here. Wait. What was that?" Chloe asks.

I respond, "What did you hear?"

"I'm not sure. Sounds like a scratching sound."

"Oh, that's probably Peanut. Let me see." I giggle.

I don't know if it's because I love Peanut so much or what, but when I see him, I don't feel so afraid. I peek in the window. It is Peanut. He's whimpering and not even wagging his tail. He looks sad. "It's okay, Peanut. It's me, Bea." I knock, but no one answers. Now, Peanut knows I'm there for sure. He's whining and barking to come out. I can see his tail wagging now. He must not be as sad since he knows I'm there.

"I need to run home and find Mr. McBean's spare key."

"Why not try the door?" Chloe says.

Is she crazy? Try the door? How about no way. She clearly hasn't seen enough scary movies to know that you should never try to open a closed door. Especially without knowing what might be hiding behind it.

"Chloe. Mr. McBean isn't home. He always looks for me and lets me in. There's no way the door would be... Chloe, don't try the handle."

To our surprise, the door is unlocked. Chloe opens it and out bounds Peanut. "Hey there, buddy, how's my favorite puppy? You're such a good boy." His tail is going a mile a minute. Gosh, he's the cutest. Well, not cuter than Tommy, but out of all the dogs around, he's the cutest.

"Watch him, Chloe, let me go grab his leash."

I go inside, but something isn't right. I yell out for Mr. McBean, but all is quiet. It's so weird he left Peanut alone. He usually takes Peanut wherever he goes. It doesn't surprise me he forgot to lock his door. We live in a tiny town, like crazy small. Being small has its benefits for sure. Everyone knows who you are. It also has some negatives, like everyone knows who you are. No one can get away with anything in this town.

Once, a few years ago, I walked to Pete's Card Shop and bought a sympathy card. I only bought it for my mom to send to her cousin, who lost her cat. I didn't even know her, never mind that she had a cat. Next thing you know, people just started showing up, dropping off casseroles. Other than Mrs. Thompson's chicken thing, they all were not too good. Now, if we need a sympathy card, we stay clear of town.

I scream, "Chloe, come quick." Something isn't right and I'm scared. I can feel my heart rate shoot up. I can feel myself shaking.

Then.

Chloe and Peanut race through the door.

"What's the matter?" she asks while she looks around the room.

She sees it, too. The living room is in shambles. There's furniture tipped over and papers scattered everywhere. Drawers are open and emptied on the floor. The picture of Mr. McBean and his wife is smashed on the floor, and glass is everywhere. It smells bad, really bad.

"What's that smell, Bea?"

"That would be a Peanut. Looks like he had an accident. That isn't like him at all, unless Mr. McBean has been gone a while. It makes no sense. What should we do? Do we call the police?"

"We're clueless at the moment, so maybe not." Chloe smartly says.

"What's this? Hey Chloe, there's a note."

I take the paper. It looks like a child wrote it, but it's clear what it says.

> *Beatrice,*
> *I am sorry. Look after the dog.*
> *Ed.*

"Ummm Bea, what the heck's going on?"

"Good question Chloe. Good question."

Now I know something is very wrong. Mr. McBean wouldn't leave such a sketchy note. I can feel panic rise inside me. This cannot be happening. I feel like I need to sit down. Bad idea. Once I sit down, Peanut thinks it is playtime. Gosh, I love this dog.

Chloe

I'm freaking out. What is going on? It was supposed to be a chill day, eating junk food, talking about boys, and listening to music. Instead, we're knee-deep in some kind of weird stuff going on. How's this even possible?

"Bea, what does that note even mean? Take care of the dog? For what? Like forever? I'm so confused."

I stand up as I nudge Peanut off of me. "Me too, Chloe, me too. It makes no sense. First, Mr. McBean has never, ever called me Beatrice. He may have the very first time I met him, but after I set him straight, he never did that again. Calling Peanut 'the dog' that's super strange, right? Why wouldn't he say take care of Peanut? Something isn't adding up."

"Peanut, hold on. Looks like Peanut wants to go for a walk. Grab the note and let's go."

We both don't know what to think, but we both know Peanut wants to get moving. We head out the door and make our way to the dog park.

Beatrice

"This is so messed up. It makes like no sense at all. Mr. McBean would never, ever leave Peanut. Another thing, he only drives, like, a little. He knows he's not too good at it and doesn't want to go back to jail or anything."

"Ummm, Bea, what the heck are you talking about? Back to jail? He was in jail? How did I not know this?"

"I'm sure you knew. It was ages ago. He went to jail for a super short time. It had something to do with someone stealing stuff. He told my dad that since he fessed up, the other guys took the time, whatever that means. I do know jail set him straight. I also know that's one reason his daughter doesn't want to be around him."

"I can't believe I didn't know any of this. You don't think he ratted the other guys out. I mean, I know snitches get stitches. Maybe he's in trouble."

"I think we need to find Mr. McBean," I answer.

"Agreed, but how?" Chloe responds.

Chloe

How did I not know Mr. McBean was in jail? That sounds fishy. I wonder if my mom knows he was in jail. She probably does, since everyone around here knows everything about everyone. Well, except for me, clearly.

We walk to the dog park, which isn't too far, and try to think what the heck is going on. Peanut doesn't seem to be too concerned Mr. McBean isn't around. Although Mr. McBean may not be too happy when he goes home and finds what Peanut left for him, which was nasty.

The dog park is next to the school. The school is deserted right now. It is summer and all. The school isn't very big, even though all grades are here. Our homeroom has only twelve kids in it.

The only one worth mentioning is Tommy. He's super cute. I know Bea likes him. Well, all the girls do. It's hard not to. He has blonde hair and blue eyes, like the ocean, and plays every sport around. I don't think he likes Bea, but I will not be the one to tell her. She only has a short time left, and it just seems mean. I actually think he likes me.

Beatrice

"There's Mr. Howard with his dog, Chip. Hey, Mr. Howard!" I yell.

Mr. Howard seems like an odd guy, but he may know something about Mr. McBean. Mr. Howard owns the auto shop down the street. He's kind of a loner since his wife passed. Talk about people bringing casseroles. She passed like a year ago, and I guarantee he is still set for dinner for a while.

"Well, hello girls. Beautiful day today, huh?"

"Sure is. Hey, Mr. Howard, did you see Mr. McBean around today?" I ask as I watch Chip and Peanut running off together.

"Mr. McBean? No, not today. Not that I remember, but I slept in a bit today and just got here. Is everything alright?"

"That's what we're trying to find out. We went to his house to walk Peanut, and he wasn't home. The house was trashed. It looks like someone was looking for something. His car was gone, too," I say.

"I'm not surprised his car isn't there. It's at my shop. He dropped it off last night around six. That's odd, he wasn't home. I dropped him off at home around seven last night. He said he was all set and would just be hanging at home and for me to call after I fixed his car. I was about to go to the shop and look into it now."

Well, that's weird. Now we know he isn't with his car and he isn't at home. Oh boy, I yelled his name, and he didn't answer. Maybe he was in there and couldn't answer. If I go there and something happened to him, and I didn't look enough, that would be bad. We need to go back and check, for sure.

"Thanks, Mr. Howard. Chloe, we need to go, now."

"Bye, girls. Let me know if you see Ed. He probably just went for a walk. I am sure he didn't wander too far."

Chloe

"Bea, are you thinking what I'm thinking?"

"I sure am. He would never go for a walk. If he did, he would never not take Peanut. You don't think he's at home, do you? Maybe he fell, and we just left him in there. We need to hustle. Let's go back and check all the rooms. Come on, Peanut, let's go."

We try to run, but Bea can't make it too far. She's struggling. I know it's the cancer. She can't do too much anymore. That makes me sad.

"Bea, let's slow it down. Running will not help, and Peanut looks too tired."

I tell her this so she doesn't think it's her. But I'm pretty sure she does. We walk the rest of the way. She always makes me go first, so when we get there, I'm the one who goes in. She's a few steps behind me. Like if a scary monster or killer is there, those few steps will save her. I don't mind so much. She has been so brave with her cancer that this seems like the least I can do.

I open the door and peek my head inside.

"Mr. McBean!" I yell.

He doesn't respond. Peanut bolts ahead and goes straight to the water bowl.

"Okay, Bea, let's go room to room together."

"I can wait here if you want me to. You know, just to be safe."

"No way, Bea. We go together. Marshmallow."

"Fine." We hold each other's hand and walk to the kitchen.

All the dishes are on the floor, broken. Now I'm getting scared, and I'm supposed to be the brave one. No Mr. McBean in here. This is too weird.

"Bea, I'm a smidge nervous about what we might find," I say.

"Me too, Chloe, me too." I hold her hand a little tighter.

We continue down the hall to the first bedroom. No, Mr. McBean isn't there either. The bathroom door is closed. I don't want to open it. I look over at Bea, and she's shaking her head no. We both know she isn't opening that door. I yell for Mr. McBean, but once again, he doesn't respond. I'm going in.

I look at Bea and whisper, "marshmallow." Bea smirks and I feel better already.

I slowly put my hand on the doorknob. I am hoping I see nothing that will blind me for life. I do not want to see a naked old guy in the tub.

Beatrice

Holy cow, there's absolutely no way I'm opening that door. I take a few steps further back and watch Chloe. If he's in there, I don't want to see anything. He could have fallen and not been able to get up. Imagine if he was in the shower and that happened. Nope, not me. I do not want to be blinded for the rest of my short life seeing a naked old guy. I'll let Chloe take one for the team.

Chloe knocks a few times on the door, nothing. My heart is going a million miles a minute. She starts to turn the doorknob. Just then, Peanut barks. We both scream. Peanut is behind us and looks like he wants to play.

"Peanut, settle down. We can't play right now. Talk about a heart attack, Chloe."

"You're not kidding."

After we catch our breath, and when I say we, I mean Chloe, since I don't think I will ever catch mine, Chloe goes to the door handle again. Slowly, she opens the door a crack and peeks in.

"Do you see anything?" *I hesitantly ask.*

"No. Maybe."

"What the heck does that mean? Is he in there?"

"No, but something is," *she says.*

This cannot be good.

"Chloe, what is it?"

When Chloe opens the door, we both scream. It's not Mr. McBean, but it looks like blood. Could it be Mr. McBean's blood? There's definitely some stuff that looks like blood on the floor. This is not good at all. Chloe kneels down on the floor to get a closer look.

"Is it blood?" I ask.

Chloe looks like she may hurl. Her face looks like it turned white. She looks like I normally look. Sick.

"Sure looks like it. It's been here a while though. Some of it's already dried."

"What do we do? Do you think he's hurt? Dead? Do we call the police? Chloe, I'm scared."

"Me too. First, let's check his bedroom. Maybe he cut himself and went to lie down. Let's not think the worst yet."

Chloe is the absolute best at calming me down. That's why we are best friends. She's always taking care of me. She's right, there's no need to panic yet. The blood could be from anything. Maybe it's only juice or jelly. Maybe he cut himself shaving. Could be anything. Please make it be anything but blood.

Chloe

He could be dead. Yup, that's blood, for sure. I'm trying not to have Bea panic, but, yeah, it's blood alright, and he could be dead. I'm freaking out, on the inside. I don't want to upset Bea any more than she already is. It sucks pretending to be brave.

"It's probably fine, Bea. Let's just close this door and pretend we didn't see it. It's probably fine."

There's no way this is fine.

"Let's go check his bedroom."

We hesitantly walk toward the last room, his bedroom. The door is open, and I peek in. I don't see anything other than another mess. Either Mr. McBean is a slob, or someone was here looking for something. The drawers are open, everything's out of the closet, and his bed is a mess. The blankets on the floor. It looks like something is under it.

"Bea, do you want to see what's under the blanket?"

"That would be a big fat NO. I do not. One hundred percent do not."

I look over at Bea, and she has her eyes closed, her hands over her ears, chanting, "marshmallow." Like that's helpful.

I don't have much choice. I slowly walk over to the edge of the blanket. I drag the corner away. The blanket moves away. This can't be happening.

"Bea? Bea?"

I grab her hand away from her ear, and she screams.

"Bea, it's okay. It's not Mr. McBean. Just some pillows. It's okay. It's not him."

Beatrice

Thank the good lord. I almost pooped myself. I'm so happy he wasn't there, dead. Now, I just need my heart to catch up with what we saw. This is insane.

First, we think Mr. McBean is missing, and then we think he may be dead. Not a good way to enjoy the 'Summer of C.' My heart can't take much more. Here I thought cancer would kill me. Now I think this may be it. This can't be happening. I have no idea what to do.

"Chloe, I think we need to regroup. I think we need to first get the heck out of here before we see anything else and decide what to do next. Do we call the police? I need to leave, like now."

"Let's get out of here and talk it out, Bea. Everything will be alright." Again, that's not what my inside voice is telling me. We are in deep now.

We find Peanut and head outside. As we walk through the house, I try not to look around too much in case I see something scary. My house is right next door, so we head there. I need to take my morning medicine, anyway. Good thing my parents are working. We get to my house, and my heart starts to slow down. It doesn't seem to be bursting out of my chest so much. This is crazy. I have no idea what to do next. I hope Chloe does.

"I just need to grab my pills. Be right back."

I go into my bedroom and sit on the bed. I need a minute to rest and think. We definitely need a plan.

After a few minutes to relax, I walk back to Chloe. I see Chloe sitting down with a notepad and paper at the kitchen table. Maybe she has a plan.

"Chloe, what should we do? Do we call the cops?"

Chloe is chewing on the end of the pen, deep in thought. She looks up at me and says, "Not yet. I think we need to review what we have so far. I don't think the cops would even get involved if he wasn't missing long enough, right?"

"This is true. Cops only get involved if a person is missing for over twenty-four hours. We know that Mr. McBean was last seen around seven last night by Mr. Howard. We should start from there. Let's start a log of what we know so far. Maybe then we can decide what to do next."

"Sounds like a good plan."

Chloe writes the word 'Missing' on the top of the page. She starts jotting down stuff we know.

- *Last seen by Mr. Howard at 7 pm on July 18th. Mr. McBean's car was at the shop.*
- *House left in shambles. Unknown if anything is missing.*
- *Peanut left alone. Could have been for a while since he pooped on the floor.*
- *Red stuff found in the bathroom. Blood? Juice? Wine? Jelly?*
- *Mr. McBean had been in prison for a short time. Maybe ratted someone out. Who?*
- *Mr. McBean left a strange note.*
- *As far as we know, no one has sent casseroles to anyone, yet. Points to no one knows for sure if he is dead.*

This doesn't seem like we know anything. We have more questions than answers.

"What should we do next, Chloe?"

"Well, I know I could use a casserole right now. I am starving. What do you have to eat around here?"

"Ha-ha, you're always hungry. I have Pop-Tarts."

"Perfect."

I go to the pantry and grab the Pop-Tarts. They're strawberry, my favorite. Another way my mom's trying to give me anything to make me happy until my time is up. Normally, she would never allow junk food to enter the house. I guess there are some perks to dying.

Chloe

Talk about nuts, this is bananas. How can a grown person just disappear? He was here one minute and gone the next. It makes no sense. I've never been so scared in my life pulling off that blanket. I thought for sure he was going to be under it, dead. Bea thought she was going to poop her pants. I think I may have.

No, probably not, but it was close.

Being in her house makes me sad. By the end of the summer, she may be gone, and I won't be coming over to hang with her anymore. It seems so unfair. She's such a great friend, and it hurts to think she won't be here. Who will be my marshmallow friend?

How can God take someone like her? I'd give anything for her to stay. Well, maybe not my life, since that would defeat the purpose of staying together, but you see what I mean. She's my best friend. We even both have the same favorite Pop-Tart. Only difference is my mom won't buy them for me. She says they aren't healthy. Maybe that's the only benefit of having a dying friend.

"I think we need to go over what we know. Where do we start? We need to find Mr. McBean and get on with our last summer." I say.

Bea responds, "I think this may be a good add to the 'Summer of C.' I love detective shows, and this is like our own personal detective show. We know at seven last night, he was dropped off at his house. We can assume all was well.

"Let's assume his house wasn't in shambles, and Peanut didn't already poop on the floor. Mr. McBean probably went in and watched TV. That's what I would've done. So, in twelve hours, he went from being okay to having his house trashed to leaving a note and vanishing."

Beatrice

This isn't a very fun day. I thought we'd be sitting on the beach about now. I have a few books I really want to read before the time comes. But, no, now we have to find Mr. McBean.

"Chloe, I think we need to go see my dad. He'll know what to do."

"I think you're right," Chloe responds.

So, my dad, he's the best. He's super smart, kind, happy, and funny all at the same time. My mom calls him the total package. I've always been his little girl. He's been at every softball game, soccer game, dance recital, and even the season of tennis practice. Based on how bad I was at tennis, he should've gotten a medal just for taking me and watching.

Most parents would've left the match the first time I hit, or should I rephrase and say, missed the ball. Not my dad. He hung on. It was painful. I'm sad that I have to leave my parents someday. I know that they'll be okay since they keep telling me that, but it's hard.

They promised me they would always be in touch, in some way, with Chloe. I think, through her, they'll always feel close to me. I wish I could grow up and work with my dad. He's the Chief of police in town. He has such a cool job. He'll know exactly what to do about Mr. McBean.

Next stop, the police station. We grab our bikes, and off we go.

The police station is super small. It doesn't have to be very big in such a small town, I guess. The station houses my dad, who is the chief, and his six deputies. There's one secretary, Marge, who handles all the paperwork. She's a tad bizarre. She's only like thirty-five or something, but she acts like an old maid. Her clothes are super old-looking, she has like ten cats, and time has not been good to her. We head inside to see if my dad is there.

"Well, Bea and Chloe, how're you two today?"

"We're doing great, Marge. We just stopped to see if my dad was in?"

"He sure is. He's in his office doing paperwork. Go on in."

"Thanks, Marge."

Chloe

Marge is a total wackadoodle. She dresses like my nana in the nursing home. She actually dyes her hair gray. It's as if she is screaming, 'I never want a boyfriend. I never want to get married. I want to be an old spinster woman.' It's crazy weird. On the other hand, Bea's dad is so nice. He's super funny. Boy, is he going to miss Bea. He may miss her even more than me – besties for the resties.

Beatrice

"Hey, Dad."

"Well, look who's here, my two favorite people. You have just made my day. What can I do for you two?"

"Dad, we have a problem. Well, a possible problem. Or maybe I'd call it an issue or a situation. It has to do with Mr. McBean."

"Oh, boy, Mr. McBean. Bea, I know you like him, and he's nice to you and Chloe, but I was going to talk to you about him when I got home tonight. He may not be as nice as you think he is. He's had a few issues with the police in the last few days that are concerning."

"Mr. McBean? That just seems wrong. What could he possibly have done that the police would be involved?"

"Like I said, I wanted to talk about it at home. It seems that he had a physical altercation with his daughter's boyfriend the other day. It was at Willie's Five and Dime. We were called, and they were both engaged in a fight. We ended up breaking it up and sending them on their separate ways. Mr. McBean had a bloody nose, probably broken.

"His daughter Rachel's boyfriend didn't look so good either. For an old guy, Mr. McBean still has some spunk in him. He also had some issues with a couple of guys he called 'business partners' sometime back. Those two guys headed to prison all because of Mr. McBean's

testimony. Twenty-five thousand dollars is still missing from that case.

"In addition, he constantly has been fighting with his other neighbor, Mr. Shaw. Mr. Shaw says Peanut is trashing his flower beds. He used to be just an old guy. Now he seems to have become a grumpy old guy."

"That doesn't seem like Mr. McBean at all. He's always so nice and calm with us, Dad."

"I know, pumpkin, but sometimes good people can get angry. I don't think it's a good idea for you two to hang around him right now, at least until we find out what's going on."

"Well, maybe what we found out about him today has something to do with the police then. It's probably a good thing we came." Chloe says.

"Okey dokey, ladies, let's just cut to the chase. What's going on?"

We sit in my dad's office and explain everything we know and what we don't know about Mr. McBean. We talk about the strange note, the messed up house, the blood-looking stuff in the bathroom, the car being at the shop, Peanut being left alone, everything.

For a few minutes, my dad just sits there, with his hands on his chin, thinking. Finally, he says,

"Well, that's pretty crazy. I can see why you're thinking something is wrong, but maybe it's all just a misunderstanding. He did have a bloody nose, so that *may explain the blood you saw. He also could have just trashed his own house, looking for something he had misplaced. Maybe he had to go to the hospital, and that's why Peanut was left alone."*

"Dad, maybe you're right. But it still feels like something isn't right. Things just don't seem to be adding up."

Chloe

This is just so strange. I had no idea he had trouble with the police. My parents are going to flip out. I certainly won't be able to go to his house anymore.

"Mr. Chase, can we show you the note he left?"

I take the note out of my pocket and hand it to Bea's dad. The note is short, and not a lot to go on.

Something's off. It's so confusing how it's written.

"Hmmm, that is strange. You think Ed, I mean, Mr. McBean, wrote it like that on purpose?" My dad asks.

I say, "We thought maybe he was trying to give us a clue. It isn't like him at all. He would never, ever call her Beatrice. Not if he didn't want her to kill him. To be clear, we didn't kill him. You know what I mean. He knows she hates anyone calling her that. We told him the day he moved in. He wouldn't have just forgotten. Maybe he's trying to tell us something. I just don't know what?"

"Oh my gosh, girls, look at this."

Bea's dad hands the note to Bea and says, "Look at the back."

Bea takes the note from her dad and turns it over. On the back is a receipt from Sunny Side Up. Sunny Side Up is the breakfast place at the corner. Why didn't we notice it before? The receipt is dated this morning at 5:00 am. Holy cow.

"Chloe, this shows he was there early this morning. He must've been alive then. Well, of course, he was alive. A dead person typically doesn't go out to breakfast. Ha-ha. So, this means our timeline just shrunk."

"Look at what it says. It shows the number of customers as three. Someone ordered three cups of coffee and three quick breakfast specials. Does he have any friends?"

"I don't think so. Not that he's ever told me. I've never seen anyone ever visit. Dad, what do you think?" Bea asks.

"I think it seems like you two should leave police business to the police and go enjoy the day. Since I know both of you hate that idea, let's think of something else. How about I send one of my deputies to his house to check it out, and you two head over to Sunnys and see if Vic knows who he was with having breakfast? Once you have a nice snack, maybe head to the beach, and enjoy this beautiful day. I'll also have Marge call the hospital and see if he showed up with his broken nose. Sound like a plan?"

"Good plan, let's go."

Bea's dad hands us some money and says, "Buy yourself some breakfast on me. You both look like you could use a snack after such a crazy morning."

"Thanks, Dad."

And off we go.

Beatrice

We head to Sunny Side Up. Sunny Side Up is a food joint that all the locals go to eat, cheap. Best milkshakes around, and their waffles are something else. Everyone loves Sunny Side. It's at the corner of First and Main Street, you can't miss it, and it has a great big sign with an egg on it out front.

It isn't a very big place for the number of people who go there. It has maybe eight booths and counter spots. It's very homey inside. Most visitors wouldn't think it was very good based on what the outside looks like, but they would be so wrong.

It's an absolutely beautiful day. The sun is so warm. This is what I'm going to miss. I doubt heaven is going to feel like this, but maybe it will. That would be nice. I would like it. I'm sure some people going to heaven like it cold. It doesn't make sense that I can have it feel like a warm summer day, and someone else can have a cold, wintry day.

What if God gets it wrong, and I end up in a chilly place? I won't like it all. Fingers crossed its warm, like the beach. Maybe once we find Mr. McBean, Chloe and I can go to the beach. It's our favorite place to hang out. Watching the waves is so relaxing. It makes me happy. Chloe too. The diner is busy. Once again, everyone knows everyone. We enter the door, and the place is hopping. Luckily, there are two seats at the counter.

"Hey girls," Vic says as she comes right over when she sees us.

Vic is the owner and face of the diner. She does it all. She only has one employee, Chuck, who cooks the food. Other than that, it's all Vic. She waits tables, cleans up, and cashes customers out, all of it. If the place is open, Vic is there. She's kind of old, maybe forty. She is really tall and thin. I think she is thin since she works all the time.

Although, if I worked in the diner, I'd probably be very overweight from eating all the delicious pies. She has dark brown hair and always keeps it in a bun. I don't think she has a boyfriend, although people in town think she is dating Chuck. I hope it's true. No one wants to be alone.

One thing I can't stand is that Vic smokes. She smokes a lot. I think it's gross. She took over the business right out of high school from her dad. It was his dad's before that. Kind of a staple in town. Everyone goes to Sunnys, especially for town gossip. If there's something going on in town, Vic will know about it.

"Hey Vic. How's everything going?" I ask.

"No complaints here. How're you feeling, Bea?"

"Good days and bad days, I guess. Today isn't too bad. Looks like it's busy in here."

"Always is. I wanted to let your mom know I have some frozen casseroles in the back, if she wants any."

Of course, casseroles. I must look a lot worse than I thought. I roll my eyes toward Chloe, and she starts to giggle. Then I start to giggle.

"Is it something I said?" asks Vic.

That just makes us giggle more.

"No, it was an old joke we were remembering, right Chloe?"

"Sure was," replies Chloe.

"Okay then, what can I get for you two? How about a piece of blueberry pie?"

"Sounds delicious. I'll take one," says Chloe.

"Not for me. I think I'll have a chocolate milkshake. My throat has a few new sores, and the cold may help it feel better."

"You got it, kiddos. Sorry, your throat is acting up. Seems yucky."

"It sure is. If it isn't my throat, then my stomach hurts. My mom is calling the doctor today to update her and see if she can give me anything to help. It's the worst."

"Sorry, Bea. I hate to know you are not feeling good. Don't forget to tell your mom about the casseroles."

And the giggling continues.

Vic comes back a few minutes later with a large milkshake and Chloe's blueberry pie. Now seems to be a good time to ask about Mr. McBean.

"Vic, we were wondering if you've seen Mr. McBean today?"

"It's Thursday, so of course I saw him. Every Thursday, like clockwork, he comes in with his old cronies, Lenny and Mike. I don't know why they keep coming since all they do is talk about the weather and politics. Boring. But it seems to work for them, I guess."

"Lenny and Mike? I know Lenny, but I never heard of Mike."

"Yeah, of course you know Lenny, everyone does. Anyone with a car for sure, he has been working at Howard's Garage for years. Mike is the guy that Ed used to work with at the mill. Good guys, but not so good at tipping, if you know what I mean."

"Gotcha. Did you notice anything weird about Mr. McBean today?" I ask.

"Other than he looked like he got in a fight again, nothing really. Although he seemed preoccupied, he kept looking over his shoulder as if he was making sure no one was looking for him. I assumed that was because he was afraid whoever gave him his bloody nose might come back, but I didn't see anyone. Why all the questions about Ed?"

"No reason. Just didn't know where he was. Peanut was left alone, and it seemed weird. Oh, that's right, Chloe. I should've left a message for my mom about Peanut. When she comes home for lunch, she's going to be greeted by ninety pounds of love she didn't know was there. Oops."

We all start laughing. Chloe and I hang out at the diner for a while, chatting and having our snack. By the time we leave, there seems to be a smidge less of a crowd, but I'm sure that won't last since the lunch crowd will be arriving shortly.

"Okay, Vic, we're off. How much is the pie and shake? Which were delightful, by the way."

"No charge for my two best customers. Have a great day. Try to stay out of trouble."

"Will do, thanks, Vic," I say.

Chloe

That was interesting. I had no idea how Bea was feeling lately. She seemed like she was feeling good. Throat sores and stomach pain? Who knew? Not me. Poor Bea. I know she gets tired easily, but that's been going on for some time. I wish I could help her feel better. I know we swore to each other that we wouldn't talk about cancer stuff, but I think she should have told me how she was feeling. Maybe her doctor will be able to help.

Beatrice

As we leave the diner, we start giggling again. Stupid casseroles. I can't believe how funny that was. I have so much fun with Chloe. I'm going to miss her most of all. Cancer sucks for everyone it affects. It seems sad that one of these times, our giggling will be our last. She'll probably find another marshmallow friend. I hope not. I wish besties for the resties was a longer time.

"Hey, girls! Have a minute? We want to ask you a question."

We both look back at the same time. I look over at Chloe and whisper, "Do you know those two guys?"

"No way, Jose. They were sitting in the diner at the booth near the back corner. I've never seen them around before."

We turn and quickly try to walk away when they are yelling again. "Hey, girls. You two. We just have a quick question."

We both stop, and Chloe, who's not afraid of anything, puts on her brave face and says, "What?"

The two men are super sketchy-looking. One is short and round with a denim jacket on. He has what I believe is supposed to be a mustache, but he doesn't know how to manage one. It's pretty sparse. He actually looks like he could be homeless. The other one has blonde hair, super skinny, and green glasses. He has a Harvard sweatshirt on. I can guarantee he did not go to Harvard. One hundred percent. I don't like the look of these two. Something is making my stomach turn. It's either Vic's yummy milkshake or these two weirdos. I vote the weirdos.

The skinny one has his hands up in front of him, like he is trying to prove he doesn't want to hurt us.

"We just have a quick question. No need to be afraid," the skinny one says.

Easy for them to say. Again, not Harvard graduates.

"What?" Chloe asks.

"We were in the diner and heard you mention someone named Ed McBean? Why are you so interested in finding him?"

"What do you care?" Again, Chloe is the brave one.

"Sometimes when someone is missing, they should stay missing, that's all."

Chloe's like, "How do you know he shouldn't be found? And who are you two anyway?"

"It makes no difference who we are. We just want you to know that looking for someone who should stay lost isn't the best idea," says the short, round one. "We know he has a daughter and we really want to talk to her, too. Any idea where she lives?"

"Nope. Sorry," I say.

We turn to leave. As we leave, I can hear the skinny guy yell, "We think you do!" We bolt.

Chloe

We go off running. We end up stopping around the corner, in the alley, mostly because Bea can't catch her breath. Poor Bea. I tell her to try to take some deep breaths. I wish I could help.

Well, that was strange. Who were those two losers? They certainly aren't from around here. Sketchy is one word to describe them. Another would be crazy, deranged, or maybe even serial killers. I wasn't hanging around to find out. No way.

Once Bea catches her breath, I peek around the corner but don't see them.

I say, "Bea, what the heck was that about? Who were those two?"

"No idea, but that was messed up. What the heck do they mean Mr. McBean shouldn't be found? That was strange. Did you see the Harvard sweatshirt? Yeah, right, Harvard?"

We both start laughing at that. Gosh, I'm going to miss seeing her face.

Beatrice

I hate how sometimes I can't catch my breath. It seems to happen more and more lately. It totally stinks. Maybe the doctors are right, and my time is almost up. I think I may cry, and then I look and see Chloe laughing. She's my best friend and always makes me feel better. I'm so lucky I have her.

"Chloe, I have no idea what that was about, but I think we need to find out. I think if we find Mr. McBean, we'll have all the answers. What do you think we should do next?"

"How about we start with Lenny? Mr. McBean's car is at the shop, right? He just met with Lenny this morning for breakfast. Maybe Mr. McBean told him something. If not, maybe we can check out the car and see if there are any clues to what happened. What do you think?"

"I think you're super smart. It sounds like a brilliant plan. Let's leave our bikes here and catch the city bus, though. I don't think I can bike all the way there. Okay?"

"Perfect. Let's go see if we can grab the next bus."

Off we go.

Chloe

The bus stop is only at the next corner. I have my eyes peeled, looking for the two weird guys, but luckily, I don't see them. We only have to wait a few minutes until the bus comes. The shop is only a few minutes away, but I can see how Bea wouldn't want to bike it. It's up a steep hill. I didn't want to bike it either.

The bus pulls over, and Stu is the driver. He's a nice kid. He went to school with my older brother, Nick. Nick and Stu used to play baseball together.

"Hey, Stu. What's up?"

"Hey there, Chloe. How are ya? How is Nick doing? I heard he's going to school to be a cop. That's pretty cool."

"Yeah, he started last year. It was that or working with my dad at the mill, and he wanted no part of that. Are you going to school too?"

"Yeah, I go to the community college. Don't want to drive a bus for the rest of my life."

"I hear ya. We're off to Howard's Garage. We want to see if Lenny's around."

"Someone has car trouble in the family? My cousin Drew fixes cars on the side."

"No, nothing like that. We're looking for Mr. McBean and heard he spoke to Lenny this morning. You haven't seen Mr. McBean, have you?"

"No. I saw his daughter Rachel's boyfriend today. He is a character, for sure. Not sure what she sees in him."

"Did he mention Mr. McBean?" I ask.

"Only that they had a fight at Willie's place. Looked like Mr. McBean got a few jabs in. Kyle had a black eye and seemed pretty mad."

"Yikes."

"Exactly."

Stu pulls out into traffic, and he drives up the hill toward Howard's place. No one else is on the bus, so that's cool. I really don't want to chat with anyone other than Bea.

Beatrice

Stu's a nice person, from what Chloe has said. Chloe's brother, Nick, is also a nice person. Truth be told, Chloe's other brother, Owen, is perfect. He is a year older than Chloe and me, so smart and super cute. He has blonde hair, the same as Chloe, and the same blue eyes. He has a few freckles across his nose, so adorable. He is kind of a nerd, too, which I really like. He's perfect.

I've had a crush on him for as long as I can remember. Chloe knows, and she says that it is gross, but man, I like him. He makes me laugh all the time. If I were going to be on this earth for a longer time, I would ask him out. He doesn't have a girlfriend, and he's super shy, so I know I would have to make the first move. Once again, cancer gets in the way.

Stu stops the bus at Howard's Garage, and we step out of the bus. Stu lets us know that after he makes his rounds, he'll be back to pick us up. Sounds good to us, although walking downhill doesn't seem too bad. It's the up that stinks.

Howard's Garage is the only auto shop in town, so all the people who live here bring their cars there. It isn't very big, it only has two bays, and Lenny is the only mechanic, but people around here don't mind waiting for repairs. Especially since Lenny usually does the job right the first time.

Lenny's a typical auto repair guy. He wears the typical dark blue uniform and has so much grease and dirt on his hands that you don't have to wonder what he does for a living. It's Mr. Howard's Garage, but Lenny pretty much runs the place. Mr. Howard only stops by occasionally to see if Lenny stopped for lunch.

By the looks of Lenny, you would stop, too. Talk about a thin man. If he weighs eighty pounds, I'd be surprised. I think Peanut weighs more. Definitely short, round stalker guy does. Lenny not only is super thin, but he also has about four teeth. I know he's good at working on cars, but other than that, I don't think he is too smart. He reminds me of a squirrel, nutty and jittery.

We walk into the garage and see Lenny at the desk.

"Hey, Lenny. How's it going?" I say.

"Oh hey, girls. It's going. What can I do for you two today?" He doesn't seem too surprised to see us there, which is surprising. It's almost like he was expecting us.

"We are looking for Mr. McBean. Have you seen him?"

"Man, that's crazy you're asking for him. I saw him this morning and have been calling him all morning, trying to find him. He hasn't answered my calls. His car is here, and after we met for breakfast, I came to start working on it. What I found was that someone broke into it. The deputy just left. I filled out a report. I thought if Ed needed it for insurance purposes, he would have it. What do you guys need with Ed?"

I say, "We went to walk Peanut, and Mr. McBean wasn't there. It was strange. No one seems to have seen him since your breakfast. We thought maybe he said something to you or Mike."

"Nothing unusual. We talked about the weather and Ed's car. He was banged up, and he told us what happened with Kyle. Other than that, nothing unusual."

"What did he say happened with Kyle?"

"Just that he went to Willie's place, and Kyle was there. They argued about Rachel. Ed thinks Kyle is a deadbeat and should stay away from Rachel. Kyle thinks Ed should mind his own business. Same old thing. I think Kyle was mad that Ed got a few licks in. I even told the deputy that maybe Kyle had something to do with Ed's car."

"That's crazy. Mind if we take a peek at Ed's car? We just want to see if anything looks out of place, and it may give us a hint of where to find him."

"Have at it. It's parked out back. Cops said they were done with it. They seem to think it was some neighborhood kids up to no good. I'm not convinced."

"Thanks, Lenny."

Off we go around back. The back lot is fenced off and seems hard for a kid to get in. Maybe Lenny left the gate unlocked. Maybe a taller person could reach up to climb over it. Either way, a young kid wouldn't be able to reach it. I sure as heck wouldn't be able to reach.

There are about six cars in the back lot. It looks like only Mr. McBean's car was touched. That seems odd if it were random kids. Especially since a few of the other cars are a lot nicer. I would have picked the Cadillac, but that's just me.

Just makes me think the break-in was personal and not so random. I share what I think with Chloe, and she agrees that it's suspicious. We walk over to Mr. McBean's car. Mr. McBean drives an old green sedan. Although one door isn't green anymore, and the car has a few dents around, I am pretty sure they are not new.

He isn't a very good driver, so that makes sense. They're old. From the outside, it's clear someone was angry. The two front door windows are broken, it has two flat tires, and someone wrote 'I know where you live' on the back window with what looks like red spray paint.

We peek in the windows, and the car is trashed. It looks like his house. The glove box is emptied, the seats are ripped, and the backup mirror is hanging off the window. Chloe calls over to me to show me something on the floor of the back seat.

"What is it, Chloe?" I say as I make my way over. Chloe is opening the back door and picks up a newspaper.

"Look at this. Its yesterday's Gazette, July Eighteenth, 1986."

"So?" I say.

"So. Look at the part someone circled," Chloe points. 'Local Man's Enemies on the Run.'

We sit down next to the car to read the article.

LOCAL MAN'S ENEMIES ON THE RUN

On Thursday, sources report that Mr. Randall Jencks and Mr. Gene Reynard escaped from Yardley Prison, where they were being held on a twenty-year sentence. They both served ten years of that sentence. Sources confirm that after the final lights out at the penitentiary on Tuesday evening, both men were accounted for.

On Wednesday morning, both men were missing. Mr. Jencks and Mr. Reynard were being held in Yardley following a brief court proceeding involving a charge of fraud. A fellow 'business partner' turned state's evidence in a court of law against the men, leading to their sentencing. That individual is a Tri-Gators local named Edward McBean. Mr. McBean was not available for an interview.

The fourth suspect remains unidentified. $25,000 is still missing. The investigation continues.

"Holy smokes, Chloe. That's crazy town. No wonder Mr. McBean was looking over his shoulder at breakfast. I would be, too, knowing two prisoners escaped and maybe after me."

"Holy cow. That's so messed up. I wonder if your dad knows about it. Do you think the two sketchy guys could be the escaped prisoners?"

"I didn't think of that. I hope not. Probably not, right? Someone would have figured that out, right? I am sure my dad is on it. Maybe we don't want to find Mr. McBean after all. Maybe the two prisoners already did, and who knows what they did to him?"

"What should we do?"

"Honestly, Chloe, I'm exhausted. I think we need a break. Would you mind if we just stop looking for Mr. McBean for a bit? I mean, he hasn't really been missing for very long, and he could still show up. Until we find out if the prisoners came this way, I vote we catch our breath, literally."

"I think that makes perfect sense. What should we do? Want to head home?"

We sit and talk about what to do next for a bit and decide to go back to my house. My mom will be coming home soon and is supposed to call the doctor. I suggest we check in with her, pack up a lunch, and head down to the beach to relax. We can take Peanut.

We can talk about Mr. McBean some more or just chill and watch the waves. We both love reading, and both are in new books that we bought recently, so I'd be fine just reading. Mine is a romance, and I really want to know what happens next. We walk to the bus stop and wait for Stu.

Chloe

I'm totally good with taking a break from the Mr. McBean situation. I know Bea is tired and probably not feeling too good, and if truth be told, I don't feel too good either. I'm sure it's stress from my best friend dying of cancer, but I can't sleep. Probably worse since we sleep on the floor all the time in each other's houses.

For some reason, when we sleep at her house, her cat, Smokey, thinks I'm a play toy in the middle of the night. The cat doesn't seem to leave me alone. It certainly has boundary issues. It's annoying, but I won't say anything to Bea since she pretty much has a lot on her mind already.

We only have to wait a few minutes for Stu to show up with our ride. Stu pulls over and opens the doors. Then it gets weird. The two sketchy-looking people from outside the diner are getting off. What are they doing here? Are they going to see Lenny? I guess if they're interested in Mr. McBean and heard Vic say he was with Lenny from the garage this morning, maybe they want to see what Lenny knows. Or they are following us.

The skinny person spots us, points, and says something to the short guy. This can't be good. I look over at Bea, and we both decide maybe it's better to walk home or rather run home.

We look at each other, grab each other's hand and say, "marshmallow."

We bolt.

Beatrice

We make a break for it. We start running pretty fast, but before long, I can't keep up with Chloe. She notices and stops to check on me.

"I'm sorry Chloe, I can't run too far."

"That's okay, Bea, it doesn't look like they're following us."

"That's crazy. What's going on? Who are those guys?"

It was more of a rhetorical question than a real question, since Chloe clearly wouldn't know either. We walk down the hill toward my house, and both seem to be thinking about what just happened. It seems weird neither one of us is talking.

Then, Chloe brings up a good point when she says that if it were those two guys who broke into Mr. McBean's car, they probably wouldn't need to go to the garage to talk to Lenny. They probably would have just walked since it wasn't too far, and they would know where they were going. Could they be the escaped prisoners? It really isn't making much sense why these two hoodlums are interested in a sweet old man. To be clear, a sweet old man who apparently does occasionally get into fistfights.

We get to my house, and thankfully, my mom isn't home yet. She won't get pushed over by a chubby puppy without knowing about it first. We run to my room and change into our bathing suits for the beach. No bikini today in case Tommy sees us again. Not taking that chance. We come in the kitchen with our bags packed with our books, and I grab us both a drink from the fridge, sit at the table, and wait for my mom.

My mom is what some would call high-maintenance. She has her hair just right, her nails done, and her makeup is flawless. She even has had a nose job, and a facelift done. She works out all the time. Everyone says my dad is a lucky man. I think he may be lucky, but his wallet probably isn't.

She's one of only three realtors in town and has the record of being the top salesperson. Probably since every single guy would die to date her and every woman wants to be just like her. It all seems fake to me.

One good thing about her being a realtor is her work schedule. She sets her own hours, so she usually is home most afternoons.

When I say she is home, I mean she's looking over her house listing book, calling clients, or working out in her home gym. She may be home, but not necessarily home, if you know what I mean. Chloe's mom is always around. She doesn't work, so she's always around the house or doing errands. She does a lot of baking, too, which is nice.

My mom comes in a few minutes later. She's always in such a good mood and is positive. It's exhausting. She would be great as a motivational speaker. I guess that's why she can sell anything.

"Hey, girls. Great day today, right? Is everything okay? You both look exhausted."

"We're okay, Mom. Just been an interesting morning."

We update her on our day, from getting to Mr. McBean's house this morning to running down the hill to home. She seems shocked at everything that went on, but says, "He's probably fine, girls. He probably went to the store or something. I wouldn't worry about him at all. It's a beautiful day out, and you should be enjoying it."

She's not wrong, but again, too much optimism. We both roll our eyes at her. She doesn't seem to notice. If it's not about her, she tends to lose interest.

"You're probably right, Mom. We thought we would pack a lunch and head to the beach."

Sometimes, it's just easier to agree than argue.

"Sounds perfect. I'm going to put on my workout clothes and work that treadmill, and then I have a few open houses to schedule."

"Are you calling the doctor's office, too?"

"Oh yeah, I'll do that today. Thanks for the reminder."

Again, if it isn't about her, she loses focus. I feel like she'll be fine when I'm gone.

Chloe

Okay, I'm sorry, but if my daughter were dying of cancer, working out would be the last thing on my mind. How could she possibly forget to call the doctor to help Bea? That's wrong on so many levels. As God is my witness, I promise I'll never, ever be that way if my child has cancer.

I'd like to punch her in the face. If I did, I would probably end up breaking my hand from hitting her, and she would just get another surgery to fix her face. I just gave her the evil eye. I feel better already.

Bea and I pack up some PB&J sandwiches, chips, and drinks and head to the beach.

Beatrice

Of course, my mom would forget about calling the doctor. It doesn't really surprise me anymore. She's always been an 'all about her kind of person.' No matter how much longer I'm going to live, I'll never be that person.

We walk to the beach, and it isn't too busy. Some local kids are playing Frisbee. I recognize them from school. Tommy is over the side of the beach talking to some girls from school, including the tramp Angela. He probably won't even notice us today. The one day it wouldn't have mattered if I wore my bikini or not.

There are a few moms with their kids building sandcastles. They're actually doing a good job. Only a few people are in the water. Chloe and I usually just hang on our towels and eat, chat, and laugh. We always have the best time. Besties for the resties.

This time, maybe because the day has been crazy so far, I sleep. I can't keep my eyes open and fall asleep super quick. I don't think we have been at the beach for five minutes, and I'm out. I even sleep thru lunch.

I wake up to Chloe pushing on my arm. I hear her say, "Bea, wake up. We have company."

Sure enough, I look up and see Tommy making his way over. Oh, crap. I'm so glad I didn't wear my bikini.

I dodged a bullet, for sure. Chloe and I both look at each other, surely thinking the very same thing.

"Hey, Tommy. How's it going?" Chloe says.

Tommy has this way about him that exudes confidence. The way he stands with his hands in his pockets, the way he flips his hair out of his eyes, even the way he walks, or should I say struts. He is so perfect, and he knows it.

"Going okay, weather's great, waves are intense, girls are pretty. What more could I ask for?" Tommy replies.

"Maybe some glasses, if that was Angela you were with. She's too trashy to be called pretty."

"I was talking about you two."

"Well then," says Chloe, "I agree."

We both start blushing as I elbow Chloe in the ribs.

"I wanted to see if you guys wanted to come tonight to the bonfire we're having. It's over by the cove tonight at dusk. Should be fun. Tons of kids from school are coming. Max and Dan are supposed to be bringing some booze. Think you want to join?"

Before I even have a chance to think about it, Chloe says, "We'll be there. Sounds fun."

Once I give Chloe the eyes, she whispers, "What? It'll be fun."

I beg to differ. I'm anxious already. What will I wear? Tommy says, "Great," and runs off. He yells over, "See you guys tonight!"

Just great.

"Chloe, I hope you know what you're doing."

"Sure do. I'm doing whatever it takes to make this the best Summer of C marshmallow."

If only she would have known her plan would backfire. I wish this was just a dream, and I was still asleep. But, no, I'm not that lucky.

Chloe

Boy, talk about being uptight. It's just a bonfire on the beach. What does she think it's going to be? It's not a big deal at all. Just a bunch of kids hanging at the beach, making s'mores, maybe a drink or two. What could go wrong?

Beatrice

Everything can go wrong. Apparently, I slept for quite a while since Chloe had lunch and finished her book. She said she didn't mind sitting alone while I slept. She said it was peaceful. She said she's going to have to get used to it before you know it. At that comment, I leaned over and hugged her. I wish I'd stop feeling how sad she will be when I'm not here. I have enough on my mind.

We pack up our stuff and head back to my house. We need to see if my mom will let us go tonight and figure out what to wear.

My mom is out when we come home. She left a note on the table that said she was running to Pete's Card Shop, which is also the pharmacy, to pick up a prescription. It's right down the street, so she shouldn't be too long. I eat my sandwich, and Chloe grabs a drink while we wait.

A few minutes later, my mom comes in. She actually ran to the store and didn't bother taking her car. I'm almost positive this was after she ran her five miles on the treadmill. No one should run that much, unless they're being chased.

"Hey, girls. How was the beach? Looks like you got a little sunburn, Bea. I can see a few more freckles."

"I'm aware. Just what I want, a few more freckles. I fell asleep for a bit before I put my sunscreen on."

"It happens. Just be more careful next time. Sunburns are your skin's enemy."

I roll my eyes and say "I will, Mom." Like that is my biggest problem in life. "Did anyone mention Mr. McBean at Pete's place?"

"Only that no one had seen him around today. Maybe no news is good news. By the way, I called Dr. Skinner, and she gave you a new med to try. It's supposed to help relieve some of the throat pain. You take it once a day at bedtime. It may make you sleepy."

"I'm already sleepy all the time, so I can't imagine it making that much of a difference."

"This is true. She also told me she wants us to come in and see her on Monday. She said that she had some interesting news she wants to talk to us about. She wouldn't go into too much detail, she just said she had something that needed to be discussed. She wants us to go in at eleven am on Monday. Sound okay?"

"Sounds good. I wonder what she has to tell us."

Chloe chimes in, "Maybe she wants to tell you that you're cured and will live forever."

"I wish," I say.

Chloe

I so hope that's the news Bea will get. Imagine if the doctor tells her it was all a mistake, and the cancer was gone. We would always be friends, go to the same college, each marry someone handsome, and raise our kids together. We could grow old together. That's all I wish for. Besties for life. Besties for the resties.

Beatrice

"Mom, a few kids from school are having a bonfire at the beach tonight. Is it okay if Chloe and I go?"

"I don't see why not. Just be safe and don't be home past curfew."

"Awesome. Thanks, Mom."

It does work out that tonight is Chloe's turn to sleep over at my house. My mom lets us do whatever we want, whereas her mom probably would say no. She is excessively cautious. It's probably the only good part of having cancer, my mom hates to say no to anything. The deal is whoever's house we are at, we need to ask permission, and that mom gets to decide for both of us. Now you know why most nights we stay at my house.

We head upstairs to plan what we're going to wear. Maybe it'll be a fun night after all.

Chloe

Thank goodness we're not at my house tonight. My mom would surely have said no. She doesn't let me do anything. Luckily, Bea's mom is so self-involved she doesn't care what we do. My mom doesn't even let us go out after dark. She's a tad crazy. I love her, but she could stand to dial down the crazy.

I think tonight will be fun. What's the worst thing that can happen?

Beatrice

After supper, we both shower, Chloe does her hair, we put makeup on, get dressed, and are ready to go. Chloe is wearing a pair of denim shorts and a cute T-shirt she found in my bottom drawer. She looks so adorable. I have on a white jean mini-skirt with a tank top. We're both bringing sweatshirts with us. We're both super excited now that we are ready to go.

Before we leave, we see my dad just coming home from work. He looks beat. We chat about Mr. McBean. We update him on what Vic told us, meeting up with Lenny, and what we found in Ed's car. We told him about the short, round guy and the skinny guy. My dad seemed concerned about who they could be. He reassures us that the two guys we describe are not what the two prisoners look like. He says he will look into who they are in the morning.

My dad told us that the deputy found little at his house, only that it looked ransacked. He knew about his car getting broken into and thought it might be neighborhood kids. He also told us he had just come from Mr. McBean's house, and he still hadn't shown up. He'll start an official missing persons report in the morning. He'll have been missing for twenty-four hours by then.

We turn to leave, and my dad yells, "Have fun, just not too much fun. Make good choices. Remember your curfew."

I grab Chloe's hand and say marshmallow. Off we go.

Chloe

The summer nights seem to get chilly, so maybe hanging with school kids at the bonfire will not only be warm but also exciting. I think Bea looks so cute with her skirt, she has a nice sunburn that helps with her being so pale. Even with only a few strands of hair, she's beautiful. She added a cute head wrap over her bald head to finish the look. So adorable.

Beatrice

We see the bonfire from across the beach, and it looks awesome. It's huge. Someone brought a radio, so there are a few people dancing around. This party rocks. There are about thirty kids around it, most making s'mores, and drinking. If my mom knew drinking was involved, she probably would have said no, even if I played the cancer card. What she doesn't know can't hurt her, right?

We know everyone that's here, so it's like a homecoming party. We head over and see Tommy with a pack of girls at his side. Angela is there, of course. She looks so trampy. Her shorts are so short you can see her butt cheeks, and it isn't pretty. I nudge Chloe, and we both start laughing. Chloe's brothers are here, too, and so is Stu. We run over to them.

"Hey, guys. This is so cool," says Chloe.

"I figured you guys would be here. I assume Mom doesn't know?" Owen comments.

"You would be correct. And no going to rat me out," replies Chloe.

"I won't, but don't do anything stupid."

"Who? Us?" And we both start laughing again.

A couple of kids see us and tell us there's beer in the cooler. Chloe and I look at each other, and both say, at exactly the same time, "What can it hurt?" That makes us laugh even more, and we head over to the cooler.

We each grab a beer and sit off to the side to chat. We talk about Angela and how gross she is, and how Tommy can do much better than a skank. We talk about Owen and how he's so nice.

I once again tell her I think he's cute and she yells, "GROSS." She yells it so loud that everyone looks over. Ugh.

We hang around and finish our beers, and Chloe goes over and grabs another one. Chloe comments, "When in Rome, right?"

After drinking two beers, we are both pretty happy and loud. We practice seeing if we can walk in a straight line. Chloe is slightly better than I am. We've been laughing and giggling all night. Neither of us wants this night to end. Then something happens.

Chloe

This is the best party ever. I've never laughed so hard in my whole life. Trying to walk in a straight line on beach sand has been a challenge, to say the least. We fell so many times. I have beach sand where beach sand should never go.

Best night ever.

Until.

Beatrice

Tommy comes our way. We nudge each other and see Tommy walking straight for us. He has three beers, one for him, and the other two for us.

"I brought you guys a drink. Saw you over here having all kinds of fun and thought I would join. Are you glad you came?"

I tell him the party was awesome, and we're so happy we came. He winks at me. I can't believe Tommy walked away from Angela to talk to us.

"So, where did Angela go? She finally got her claws away from you?" Chloe asks.

"Ha-ha, hilarious. We're just friends. She just likes my abs and my witty personality."

"Ha-ha, that must be it," Chloe says.

We have our beer and continue to talk to Tommy for some time. He really does have a witty personality. I could stare at him all day.

After we finish our beers, Chloe says she has to pee. She said she was going to run back to my house to use the bathroom and would be back. I gave her the eyes that screamed marshmallow, but she said she had to go. Honestly, I don't know how she could leave when I could barely walk straight. There's no way I could've left now. Chloe ran off to my house.

Right after she left, Tommy reached for my hand and pulled me up. I stumbled and fell into him. He started laughing and said not to worry about it. He said it happens to everyone when they first start drinking. I was slightly mortified, but truth be told, I didn't hate landing in Tommy's arms.

Tommy said he had something to show me over the dunes. He grabbed my hand and helped me walk with him. I felt so safe and protected. He smelled like vanilla.

We walk over to the dunes, and he asks me to sit next to him. It's a dream come true to sit next to Tommy. He looks so happy to be by my side.

Tommy reached over and touched my lips, he pulled me toward him and kissed me. It was amazing. This was my very first kiss. It was soft and gentle. I couldn't believe it. I wish Chloe were here so I could tell her. Well, not yet. I want another kiss.

"Is it okay that I kissed you?" Tommy asks.

I am so happy. I know I am blushing. I can feel my face turning red. I am so excited right now. This is a dream come true.

"Heck, yes. Can we do it again?"

"I can't think of anything I would like better," He says.

Tommy pushed my back to the ground and started to kiss me again. I'm the luckiest girl around. That must mean something coming from someone who has cancer. Tommy continues to softly kiss me. He tells me I'm so beautiful. He's sliding his hands up and down my body. I am playing with his hair and rubbing his back. It just feels right. I want to stay like this forever.

Until I didn't.

Tommy puts his hand up my shirt. He reaches for my bra and pushes it aside. He cups my breast with his hand and starts to kiss me hard. He pushes his tongue into my mouth, making it hard for me to say no. I finally get a chance and yell STOP!

He says, "You know you like it."

What is happening? This isn't what I want. I feel powerless. It feels like he is being so aggressive and pushy. What the heck?

"No, I don't. You need to stop." I gasp.

"Come on. I promise you'll like it."

He pushes himself on top of me. He grabs both of my hands with one of his hands and holds them over my head. He's pushing his tongue into my mouth. He tears my shirt off. He's hurting me. I can't yell, and I can't fight. It must be the beer. I feel like I am sitting off to the side watching a movie. This can't be happening.

I squirm to try to get away from him. He punches me in the face and tells me to stop fighting him. He says it's going to happen and to be quiet. I can't believe this is happening. I cry, but I don't even think he notices.

Tommy puts his hand up my skirt and starts to pull on my underwear.

I scream, "STOP." The music is loud, and we're a ways away from everyone. No one hears me. He punches me again. I can taste blood. He says he'll punch me again if I don't stop screaming.

"Please stop," I say. The words are hard to come out, with blood filling my mouth.

"You're going to love it," he says.

I'm lost. I can't fight anymore. I can't help but lay there and cry. Why is this happening?

Tommy rips off my underwear. I hear him unzipping his pants. I am powerless. This can't be happening. Tommy keeps saying to stop fighting and enjoy it. How can I enjoy something that hurts and that I don't want?

Tommy stops and yells, "What the fuck, man?"

He gets yanked off me, and I see someone punching him in the face. Tommy gets pushed into the sand, and someone is kicking him. I can't tell who it is. It's too dark.

Tommy screams, "Leave me alone."

I hear his attacker say, "You leave her alone. Get the hell away from her."

Tommy yells "Gladly! She would have been a lousy lay, anyway. She should just die already. I was trying to do her a favor since no one else wants her. Bitch."

Tommy struggles to get up and stumbles away.

I am mortified. I have no shirt on, I have blood running down my chin, my face is hurting, and my *whole body hurts. Then I saw who it was that helped me. Owen.*

After Tommy leaves, Owen comes over, takes off his sweatshirt, and helps me put it on. He helps me up and helps me fix my skirt. He uses my ripped shirt to wipe off the blood from my face.

I lean on him and just start crying. He puts his arms around me and says he's so sorry for what Tommy did. He tells me it wasn't my fault. He says that Tommy has a reputation for taking what isn't his. He lets me stand there, holding on to him until I can stop crying.

He says, "Let's go and find Chloe and get you home."

Owen, my hero.

Chloe

I've been walking around the bonfire looking for Bea but can't find her. Maybe she felt sick from the beer and went off somewhere to puke. That's pretty much what I had to do on the way to her house. With God as my witness, I am never going to drink again. It is terrible.

I sit off the side of the bonfire and wait to see if Bea comes back. After what feels like forever, I look up and see my brother and Bea walking over. Owen is practically holding Bea up. She has on his sweatshirt. What the heck? Then I see her face. I see she is crying and has blood on her face. Her eye looks like it's swollen.

"Oh my God, Bea, what happened?" I yell. "Owen, what happened? How did she get hurt? Did she fall?"

"Chloe, she's going to be okay. Just take her home and put some ice on her eye. It's her story to tell, and I'm sure she will tell you what happened. Right now is probably not the best time to go into details. I promise she'll be okay. I'll take care of everything," Owen explains.

"I can't believe this. All I did was run to her house to pee. Are you sure she'll be okay?"

"I'm positive. Just get her home, and I'll handle it."

My brother hugs Bea and hands her off to me. She whispers don't go as he's pulling away from her. He leans toward her, kisses her forehead, and says, "It'll be okay, Bea, promise."

Off he goes.

I put my arm around Bea, and we walk toward her house slowly. When we get halfway to her house, I say, "Do you want to talk about it?"

Bea says, "No, not yet. I just want to get home and take a shower. Can we talk about it later?"

"Of course. Let's get you home."

We get to her front door and I open it and step inside first to see where her parents are. I'm sure Bea doesn't want to have to explain what happened to them now, or ever, for that matter.

Her dad is asleep in front of the TV on the couch. I can hear the treadmill running in the other room. I grab Bea's hand and guide her to her bedroom. Her parents are oblivious.

We go into her room, and she grabs her pajamas and heads for the shower. I can't believe something happened to my best friend. She's going through so much already. She doesn't deserve to have more bad things happen. I creep down the stairs to the kitchen and grab a bag of peas from the freezer. I make it back to her bedroom unnoticed. I get in my pajamas and wait for Bea.

Bea comes in, and I help her get into her bed. She looks better with the blood off her face. It doesn't look like she has a bloody lip. I give her the frozen peas to place on her swollen eye. I lay next to her and put my arm around her.

I hear her whisper marshmallow.

We both fall asleep quickly.

Beatrice

I wake up and see Chloe showered, dressed, and ready for the day. She's sitting on my beanbag chair reading. She sees me getting up, comes over, and sits next to me on the bed. I tell her what happened with Tommy.

I tell her how Tommy pushed himself on me, how he punched me, what he tried to do. I tell her how I bit the inside of my cheek and how much it still hurts. I tell her how he ripped my shirt off and my underwear. I tell her the horrible things he said about me.

I cry through the entire story. I'm reliving it all over again, and it hurts just as much. I tell her how Owen came to my rescue. Chloe listens without talking and lets me get it all out. When I'm done, she hugs me and tells me everything is going to be all right. I believe her when she says it.

We pinky swear promise never, ever, no matter what, to ever drink beer again until we are old, like thirty-five or forty years old. No drinking period. By then, we both think we will be old enough to know how to handle it.

We both realize I won't be around at age thirty-five, but neither one of us says it out loud. We commit to the rule that if either of us drinks beer before we are thirty-five, that person will have to walk into town with no shirt on. We both know no one wants to do that.

I get up and get dressed for the day. I look in the mirror, and my eye is black and blue. It's not swollen, but it doesn't look too good. Chloe uses some of her makeup to cover it. It's not perfect. We decided I should wear sunglasses and maybe no one will notice. We head downstairs to see what we can have for breakfast.

My dad is getting ready to leave. He looks up on his way out and sees us.

"Hey, girls, I didn't even hear you come in last night. What's with the glasses, Stevie Wonder?"

"Hilarious, Dad. The light seems to be bothering my eyes today for some reason. The glasses seem to help."

"Very hip," he says.

"Your mom is at her open house, and I'm heading into work. Before I go, a quick question, were there a lot of people at the bonfire last night?"

"Maybe twenty-five, thirty. A good crowd."

"Did you guys see Tommy Myer at the bonfire last night?"

"He was there. Why?" I ask. I'm scared of where this is going. What does my dad know? Does he know what happened?

"His mom called the station this morning and said Tommy never came home last night. That isn't like him at all, so his mom says. She's worried. I'm heading into the station to meet some of the deputies and start a search around. Any idea where he may be?"

Both Chloe and I say no, maybe a little too quickly. My dad doesn't seem to notice. Not very cop-like to not see that was sketchy, but whatever.

My dad asks what we are up to and tells us that Mr. McBean still isn't home. He went and checked again this morning. He said that since it was over twenty-four hours that he was missing, he was going to fill out a missing persons report. He said that he called his daughter, Rachel, but she didn't answer. He also says he's going to take Peanut with him to work. He makes it sound like he doesn't really want to, but we all know he loves that dog.

"Would you girls go over to Rachel's house this morning and tell her I'm filling out the missing persons report? See if she knows anything. I would do it or have one of my deputies do it, but with the Tommy issue, we just won't have time."

"No worries, Dad. We're on it."

"Thanks, girls. And Bea, you probably want to remember to tell Dr. Skinner about the eye sensitivity you're having when you see her tomorrow."

"Okay, Dad. Love you. I'll let you know what happens at Rachel's."

"Sounds good. Love you more."

My dad grabs his jacket and heads out. He turns back and says, "Here, take this and go out to breakfast on me.

Vic loves seeing you guys." He hands us $20. Breakfast decisions for today have been determined.

Chloe

That was close. I wonder if he really thought nothing had happened with Tommy. Now Tommy is missing. Crap. I wonder what happened. I wonder if Owen found him and beat him up some more. I wonder if he thought Bea would turn him in to the cops and decided to run.

He's a major jerk. I can't believe he attacked Bea. She is fragile and sick, and he has the nerve to take advantage of her. What a scumbag. I'm glad he's missing. I hope something bad happened to him. He deserves it. If I see him, I may kill him myself.

We probably should have told Bea's dad what happened with Tommy, but with Mr. McBean still missing, we don't have time to look for someone who we are happy is missing.

Beatrice

We grab our helmets and go out to grab our bikes. We decide to head to Rachel's house first and then move on to breakfast. On our way, we talk about what to order. It only takes a little while to reach Rachel's house. It's just on the outskirts of town.

Not a very nice neighborhood, somewhat dumpy. We know we'll have to lock up our bikes unless we want to have them stolen, which we definitely don't want to happen. We lock our bikes up to the front door handrail, and Chloe knocks on the door.

Both of us aren't really looking forward to talking to Rachel. She seems somewhat mean, and we are both slightly terrified of her being angry and taking it out on us. After what seems like forever, the door opens.

Rachel is still in her pajamas and doesn't look like she has showered in quite a while. She's holding a can of beer in one hand and a cigarette in the other. To say the house reeks would be an understatement.

"Hi, Rachel. How's everything going?" I ask.

"Fine. What do you guys want? If you're selling something, I ain't buying. My money is tied up in investments." She giggles.

"No, we're not selling anything. My dad asked me to come by and see you. He doesn't have time this morning and wanted me to give you a heads up."

"I didn't do it. I didn't do anything. Tell your dad to leave me alone. I haven't left the house in days. Well, only to buy smokes and booze, but nothing else. If he thinks I did something, he needs to prove it. I am not going to jail again."

"Hold on, Rachel. It has nothing to do with you doing anything wrong."

"So, it's Kyle? Is that the issue? My dad is the one who instigated the fight. Kyle was only defending himself. Tell your dad ---"

"No, Rachel, it's not Kyle," I interrupt.

"What the hell do you want with me, then?"

"It's your dad. No one has seen or heard from him since yesterday morning. No one seems to know where he is. My dad wanted you to know and see if you knew where he was?" I explain.

"How the hell would I know? He isn't here. He probably is afraid Kyle is going to come after him. I wouldn't blame Kyle if he did. My dad needs to stay out of my relationship with Kyle. I love Kyle, and if I had to choose, I would choose Kyle. I am glad he is rotting in hell."

"Okay then. Guess you have no info. Well, my dad wanted you to know he's filing a missing persons report on your dad. He'll let you know if he hears anything about him."

"Tell your dad not to bother. I don't care what happens to him. I'm glad he's gone. The only one that would give a shit that he's dead is his mom. And she is so old, she probably doesn't even remember who he is."

Rachel then flicks her cigarette at us, turns, and slams the door closed.

"Well, that was pleasant," Chloe says.

"Jeepers Crow. What was that about? She is a total wacko. You know what was weird? She talked about her dad as if he was dead. Did you notice? She said she didn't care if he was rotting in hell. It's like she already knows we won't find him. I wonder if she and Kyle did something bad."

Chloe says, "I thought the same thing. It does seem to make sense. In crime shows, you're supposed to follow the money and I'm sure his stuff would all go to her. He has no one else, right?"

"And where the heck is his mom? I thought he was old. His mom must be like eight million years old by now. How is that even possible she is still alive?"

"Exactly," Chloe responds.

Chloe

There is no way Mr. McBean's mother could still be alive. She must be crazy old.

I say, "I honestly think we need to find her. If she's that old, she should be in a records book as the oldest person on the planet."

We both crack up laughing. So much so neither of us can seem to stop. I'm going to miss this the most.

Beatrice

Oh my goodness, that's hilarious. We both agreed we needed to find her just so that if she made the records book, we could tell everyone we were there. How great would that be? We decide to go to Sunnys and get breakfast. On the way, we continue to laugh hysterically.

Sunnys is super busy today. It's Sunday morning, after all. Most of the booths are taken by screaming kids and their families. We hop on two of the open stools at the counter, and Vic immediately heads over.

"Hey, girls. How are you two doing today? It's a beautiful day today."

"Hey Vic, we're doing great. It is beautiful outside. Hey, Vic, do you know if Mr. McBean's mom is still alive?"

"You guys still looking for him? I figured he would have shown up by now. His mom? Yeah, she's alive. She's up at Oakfield Nursing Home. The place is up on Park Street. Been there for years. Ed updates me sometimes about how she's doing. She is a little forgetful, but not too bad, I guess."

"She must be old?" we say at the same time and start to laugh uncontrollably.

"She isn't young, that's for sure. I think she's about ninety. Ed is around sixty-five."

"Mr. McBean is only sixty-five? Oh boy, we thought he was around eighty." The laughter continues. This time, Vic is laughing too.

We both decide on chocolate chip pancakes and chocolate milk. Vic tells us it'll be right up. We both sit and talk about Mr. McBean. We both agree Rachel and Kyle seem mighty suspicious. We think something may have happened to Mr. McBean, and Rachel knows more than she's saying.

We also talk about the two sketchy-looking guys that keep showing up. They certainly seem up to no good. Maybe he did just go under the radar to get away from those two guys or his daughter and Kyle. We need more information. While we are talking, Lenny shows up and sits down next to us.

"Hi, Lenny. How goes the auto repair business?"

"Always cars to repair. Always busy. Grabbing a bite and heading back. Too much work to not be there on a Sunday. What are you guys up to? Any developments on Ed?"

"Not much on Mr. McBean. My dad is filling out a missing persons report. We talked to Rachel, but she doesn't know anything, still no signs of him. Vic told us where his mom was, so we may go up and see if we can talk to her. Did you hear anything from him?"

"I haven't heard anything. I'm getting worried. He's my best friend, and I wish I knew where he was. I'm not surprised Rachel knew nothing. Ed didn't talk to her very much. Their relationship was nonexistent. She's always drinking and smoking pot. Ed washed his hands of her. Not sure how much you'll get out of his mom. She's usually very confused."

"Rachel did look a little rough, that's for sure. Do you have any idea where Mr. McBean could be?"

"Nope. No idea at all. He doesn't go very far," he replies.

"Hey, did you know those two sketchy-looking guys that went to see you yesterday after we left?"

"What two guys? I didn't see anyone after you two left. No one stopped by the shop all afternoon."

"Really? When we were going to the bus, two guys were getting off and heading toward the garage."

"You must be wrong. I didn't see anyone," he replies.

We pay our bill and head outside at the same time as Lenny. He stops to light a cigarette. I stop dead in my tracks. Lenny is using a silver lighter that I've seen a million times, belonging to Mr. McBean. He never let it out of his sight. His dead wife gave it to him on their wedding anniversary. Well, before she was dead, of course. It has a special message engraved on the side. It says, 'You are the light of my life.' I can clearly see the engraving on the lighter in Lenny's hand.

"Lenny, where did you get that lighter?" I ask.

"This old thing? Had it forever. A gift from my cousin. Why?" he answers.

"Just wondering. Gotta go, have a good day."

I grab Chloe's arm and run toward our bikes. I need to get out of here and fill Chloe in on what's going on.

Chloe

"What the heck, Bea? What is going on?"

We jump on our bikes and head to the park.

"Bea? What is it? What happened back there?"

Once we stop and I catch my breath, I explain what I think.

"Chloe, did you see what Lenny had?"

"A cigarette? Oh, wow, so scary. What's the big deal?"

"No, Chloe. He had Mr. McBean's special lighter. The one his wife gave him, and he never let out of his sight. Why would he have it? Why would he lie about it? Do you think he did something to Mr. McBean?"

"That's crazy, Bea. Are you listening to yourself? They're best friends. Maybe Mr. McBean left it in his car, and Lenny picked it up to hold on to it for him. Maybe Mr. McBean forgot it at the restaurant, and Lenny picked it up for him."

"Then why lie about it and say his cousin gave it to him? It's Mr. McBean's. One hundred percent. What about the two guys that got off the bus? We both know they went to the shop. Why would he lie about that?" Bea says.

"Maybe they didn't go to the shop. We didn't see them go there. We just saw them get off the bus. I think you're just looking for something when something isn't there."

"Maybe, maybe," I hesitantly reply.

Beatrice

I still think it's weird that Lenny has his lighter. That makes zero sense. Mr. McBean would never part with it. Something is up with that, for sure.

We decided the next step should be to talk to Mr. McBean's mother. Even though she's crazy old, she may be able to tell us something to help us find him. We get on our bikes and head to Oakfield Nursing Home. The nursing home is about six blocks from Sunnys, so it doesn't take us long to get there. Thankfully, its close since I'm already tired and getting a headache.

Oakfield Nursing Home is a two-story brick building with a circular driveway. Not too sure why they made it circular, since I think once you're brought here, you probably never leave. We lock our bikes out front and go in.

"Well, hello there, Bea. It's so nice to see you. How's that handsome dad of yours?" the receptionist asks.

Oh, boy, I didn't realize Helen was the receptionist. Ugh. I probably wouldn't have gone in. It is no secret that she is obsessed with my dad.

"Hi, Helen. My dad is fine. Still happily married to my mother."

"Shucks. That's a shame. You never know if it ever doesn't work out."

"I know. I'll let my dad know you're available."

"Thanks, hun. Now, who do we have here?"

I introduce her to Chloe. More people in town seem to know me just because my dad is the chief. Bothers me sometimes. I can't do anything wrong in town, or my dad is the first to know. There are eyes everywhere. Ugh.

"Well, hello, Chloe. Nice to meet you. What can I do for you two young ladies today? Seems too nice of a day to be visiting this place."

"It is nice outside. We're here to see if we can talk to Mr. McBean's mother. We heard she lives here."

"Millie? Is she some type of celebrity or something? You two are the second set of people to come in today to see her. The other two I wouldn't let in. They weren't even a hundred percent sure she was here. I told them to take off, or I'd call the police."

"Was one wearing a Harvard sweatshirt?"

"How did you know? Do you know them?"

I reply, "No, we don't know them. Just have seen them around town the last few days asking about Mr. McBean. They look kind of weird."

"They sure did. Maybe I should have called the police?"

"I'll let my dad know. We already told him they were around asking questions. I'm sure he will want to see what they are up to."

"Sounds good. You two, I will let you in. Only because I could be your new mommy someday." She laughs as if it's super funny.

I don't find it funny at all. More like terrifying.

"Yeah, maybe. We can only hope." I say, as I roll my eyes.

She continues to laugh some more. I'd kill myself before she became my new mom.

Supposedly, in high school, Helen and my dad dated. I don't think for very long, since my dad says it was not a big deal, but clearly, he left an impression on Helen. I want to tell her to get over it, but sometimes it is easier to just roll your eyes and move on.

"Millie is out on the patio with one of the other patients, Carl. She is the one with the purple ribbons in her hair. I'll buzz you guys in, but you should know she isn't having a very good day today. More forgetful and confused than ever."

"Thanks, Helen."

We head in.

Chloe

We head inside the glass doors, and boy, does this place stink. It's horrible. It smells like poop, pee, yucky food, and vomit. It smells like old people. I thought Rachel's house smelled gross. This is like 500 times worse. I think I may be sick. Bea has her shirt collar pulled over her nose. I try it, too, but it doesn't really help.

How can people work here? They must have zero sense of smell. We head to the patio and there are about six people in wheelchairs. A few look like they are sleeping. A few look dead. Wait, no, that one just took a breath, still alive. The other one, though, the verdict is out.

Two people are sitting at a table with coloring books. The woman is really old, with white hair with purple ribbons in it and wrinkled skin. She has an odd look in her eyes, like staring off at nothing. The guy she's with is trying to direct her to the coloring books. That must be Millie and Carl. We head over to find out.

Beatrice

We walk over, and I introduce us. They are Millie and Carl, according to the guy. Millie hasn't spotted us yet. She looks up and says, "Who are you? Do I know you? Aren't you two precious? Do I know you? Are you here to take me to the dance?"

We say hello and ask if we can sit with them. Carl says, "Of course, have a seat."

Millie looks up and says, "Who are you? Do I know you? Aren't you two precious? Do I know you? Are you here to take me to dance?"

Chloe and I just look at each other. This may not go so well. Carl sees us look at each other and says that Millie isn't having a very good day. He asked us why we wanted to talk to her.

I say, "We had a few questions about her son Ed."

Millie looks up and says, "Ed? Who is Ed? I don't know no one named Ed. Who are you? Do I know you? Aren't you two precious? Is this Ed fellow going to the dance, too?"

Carl responds to Millie, "Millie, you know Eddie. He is your son, remember?"

"Oh, Eddie. Yes, he's my son. What a good boy. I just dropped him off at school. He's in first grade. What a good boy he is."

Carl tries to explain to Millie that Ed is a grown-up now. She doesn't seem to be listening. She looks up at us and says, "Who are you? Do I know you? Aren't you two precious?"

Oh, boy, this isn't going to be easy. She has lost her mind. We just smile and humor her. Carl tells Millie to work on her coloring and pulls us off to the other side of the patio to talk quietly.

"I am sorry about that. She isn't having a very good day today. Some days are better than others, but lately, they're few and far between. I hate to see her like this. We've been friends since grade school. She was always such a smart woman. Married to Ed's father for fifty years until he passed of cancer. Just a nice family. It's sad she is as she is now. What do guys need to know about Ed? I have known him since he was born. Maybe I can help."

"That would be great. We have been trying to find Ed. He hasn't been around since Thursday morning. He was at Sunny Side with his friends and then vanished." I say.

He responds, "Vanished? That is odd. I mean, I know he has had some issues lately, but vanished? Odd. Are you sure he just didn't go away? Does he have his car?"

We explain his car is at the shop, his place was ransacked, and how he left Peanut. We told him that my dad filled out a missing persons report and that we were worried. We explain no one has seen or heard from him. We told him we thought Millie might know something.

"Millie certainly wouldn't know anything. She doesn't even remember she has a son half the time. It does seem strange that he would just go missing. Has anyone checked his fishing cabin?"

"Fishing cabin? He has a fishing cabin?" Chloe says.

"He did have one. On Hemlock Lake. It's in the woods. From what I remember, there's an orange marker about halfway down Point Street, and the cabin sits back in those woods. If it's even still there. That was years ago. I know you can't see it from the street. You have to hike in. Maybe your dad could find out if he still has it or if it's even still upright."

"We'll check. That's interesting. Maybe my dad will know, is right. The issues you mentioned him having. What kind of issues?"

"Well, I know he just had problems with Kyle. Not sure what went down, but I know fists were flying. He also had the whole fraud thing. That was something for sure."

We explain what we knew about the Kyle fight and our meeting with Rachel and all she says. He mentioned he wasn't really surprised by Rachel taking Kyle's side. He said Ed didn't really have a very good relationship with Rachel. Rachel had been into drugs, and that ended up tearing them apart.

"Can you tell us about the fraud thing? I know the two prisoners escaped, and there's money missing, but not much else."

"That was a long time ago. Ten, twelve years ago. From what I heard, four people were involved in the fraud. One night at the bar, they decided it would be good to take the mill for some money. They thought the mill was making money hand over fist and treating their employees pretty bad.

"One of the people-what was his name? Oh yeah, Randy. He worked in the mill hiring workers. The other person, Gene, worked on the floor with Ed. I am not sure who the fourth person was. We always assumed it was a person who worked with Ed at the mill. Their plan was to make fake worker profiles and cash their bogus checks.

"The plan worked for a while. No one seemed to see the missing money. Randy would set up fake personnel hiring records, and Gene would punch in the person's time card. Ed and the other person were responsible for getting the checks and cashing them. Ed was the one who drove to the next town to get the checks from the post office box they had set up. He was the only one with a reliable car.

"It was a poor plan from the get-go. Ed wanted to stop, but the others wanted to keep the plan going. Ed threatened to go to the cops, but got beat up instead. Ed *ended up in the hospital with a few broken ribs, a black eye, and a broken arm.*

"This all happened while the cops, with the mill auditors, were in the process of figuring out what was going down. Your dad turned in Randy and Gene. He never would say who the fourth person was. No one knows for sure. The two people got twenty years. Apparently, this was not their first time in front of a judge. It wasn't their first rodeo. Ed just got probation since he cooperated with the authorities, and it was his first offense."

"Wow, Carl. I cannot believe that Mr. McBean was involved with something like that. That's crazy. We had no idea what had happened. So, no one knows who the fourth person was? And what happened to all the stolen money?"

Carl responds, "No one knows the fourth guy. We all have our suspicions, but nothing could ever be proved. I think it's still an open case. The money has never been found. Some people believe Ed still has it somewhere, and others think the fourth person has it. That's a lot of money to be sitting around somewhere."

"Sure is," I respond. "Who do you think the fourth guy was?"

"Like I said, there is no proof at all, and some people argue it was only just the three of them. That maybe Gene and Randy made the other person up to put the

blame on someone else. I keep thinking it was this guy named Mike. He worked with Ed at the mill, and as far as I know, they are still pretty friendly."

"Mike? I think that may be the person he was having breakfast with at Sunny Side yesterday morning. It was Mike, Lenny, and Ed. Must be the same, Mike."

"That seems right. Lenny, huh? I am not too sure about him. He's an interesting character."

"How so?" I ask.

"Just a bit of an oddball. Nevertheless, I don't think he's smart enough to be involved with anything. He's just a local grease monkey who seems a bit special, if you know what I mean?"

We both giggle. Lenny does seem a little bit special. We thank Carl for all the information and tell him we'll keep him posted. We say our goodbyes and finally get away from the disgusting smell. Once we make it outside, we both take a long, deep breath, although I don't think the smell will ever leave us.

Chloe

Poor Millie. I feel bad that she doesn't know who anyone is. That is so sad. I definitely hope that never happens to me, or anyone I know for that matter. If my mom didn't even know she had me, I think I would die.

Maybe that's the upside to Bea having cancer. She never has to go through having it happen to her or anyone she knows. I don't think there are many upsides to having cancer, so maybe I'll just think about that when the time comes and make myself feel better.

We decide to see Bea's dad and update him on what's going on. Something tells me this is getting crazier and crazier as time goes by.

Beatrice

All this stuff with Mr. McBean is getting weird. It's time to go see my dad and find out what to do next. We grab our bikes and head to the station. It's not too long of a ride, and the breeze feels nice on the ride. I feel free. I wish this feeling would last forever.

We get to the station, and Marge is at her desk. She greets us and tells us that my dad is in a meeting and will be out in a few. She tells us to head into his office, and when she sees him, she'll send him in.

We head to his office. His desk is messy, which surprises me since, at home, he is actually neat for a guy. We find Peanut lying on the floor, looking super cute. We both sit next to him and pet him while we wait. His tail won't stop wagging.

Chloe and I sit next to Peanut and talk about Mr. McBean and Tommy. We both want to know if Tommy was found and what happened to him. Although, I would prefer him to never show his face in town again. I hate him and his stupid face.

My dad heads into his office about ten minutes later.

"Hey, girls! Aren't you a welcome sight? It's been the worst day. Talk about busy. I haven't even had time to grab a coffee. How're you guys? Did you see Rachel and let her know about the missing persons report?"

I reply, "We did. She's a weird one. She wants nothing to do with her dad at all. She actually said she was glad he was gone. It was strange that she talked about him in past tense, too. Like she knew he wouldn't come back."

"That is bizarre. Was Kyle there too?" My dad asks.

"No, we didn't see him. We ran into Lenny at Sunnys. He had Mr. McBean's lighter with him. I asked about it, and he lied and said it was a gift from his cousin and he had it for years. Mr. McBean would never have the lighter out of his sight. It made no sense why he lied."

"Maybe he misunderstood the question. Lenny and Ed have been friends for such a long time. I can't see Lenny being involved in him missing."

We explain the conversation we had with, well, to be clear, we didn't have with Millie, but we had with Carl. We told him about the two sketchy guys showing up at the nursing home.

We told him about the missing money and that maybe Mike was involved. We tell him that maybe Mr. McBean has a fishing cabin. We even tell him how Millie didn't even know she had a son, and when she realized it, she thought he was still in school.

One thing about my dad is that he's a great listener. I guess, being the chief, you need to be good at paying attention to all the details. We spend about a half hour telling him everything we know.

He makes no comments until we're all done, then he looks at us and says, "Wow. That's a lot going on. I think it is best if you two stay out of it from now on. This may be going down a bad road, and keeping you safe is my main priority.

"Before you guys take off, let's go over each thing you brought up, so I can be sure of what I heard. First, I doubt Rachel or Kyle are smart enough to plan and do something to Ed. They can barely keep themselves fed and clean. They're probably too busy buying booze and cigarettes and who knows what else.

"That being said, I feel we should still be on the lookout for what they're up to. Next, Lenny. I just can't imagine him doing something to his best friend. However, I will say that money is a big motivation, so we need to keep our eyes on him, too.

"Next, everything Carl told you seems true. The money is still missing. The two prisoners have yet to be apprehended. All stations were notified via the national bulletin to be on the lookout for them in the area. I'll have my deputy take a ride out to Mike's place and see if he knows anything.

"I've also heard the rumors about Mike being involved with the fraud at the mill. As far as Ed's fishing cabin, that I'm not sure about. I'll have Marge see what she can find out.

"Lastly, the two people that keep showing up. Stay away from them. I don't know what they're up to, but it doesn't seem to be anything good. I'll have my team see if they can find them and find out what they want."

"Thanks, Dad. I feel better knowing there's a plan to find Mr. McBean. He's always been nice to me and Chloe. We don't want to see him get hurt."

"No problem at all. It's my job, after all, and I am a trained professional. With that, I think you guys have done more than enough today and need to leave it in my hands. Head home, grab some lunch, and head to the beach. We can talk about any updates I have for you at dinnertime. Mom said we're having pizza from Rizza's tonight."

"Perfect. We love their pizza. We'll head to the beach. Thanks, Dad. You're the best." I can already feel my mouth watering for the pizza.

We start toward the door, and I turn and ask, "By the way, any news on Tommy?"

"Still missing. We're reaching out to some of his friends, to see what they know. Apparently, he was pretty drunk. We think maybe he ended up crashing at one of his friends' houses. That's what we're hoping, anyway. Did you notice him with anyone in particular last night?"

"Nope," we both say, maybe a tad too fast. We head out the door and go toward our bikes.

As we walk outside, I whisper to Chloe, "You don't think my dad will find out what Tommy did to me last night?"

Chloe

I'm so glad we can go to the beach. We both need a break from all this drama. I mean, I like Mr. McBean, but he is getting in the way of Summer of C. All I wanted was to spend a quiet, calm summer with Bea. She doesn't need so much stress in her life right now. She has enough to worry about.

Now she has a doctor's appointment tomorrow to discuss her cancer. I'm scared. I've been praying so much for them to be wrong, but I also understand science and that there are many people with bigger prayers to be answered. Not sure if my prayers are even being heard.

We head to Bea's house to pack up a lunch and get our bathing suits. I don't even know why we bother putting on bathing suits, since neither one of us likes to swim. We never cared to learn. Kind of crazy when we live so close to the beach.

I think the ocean is terrifying. There are so many creatures that can kill you. No, thank you. I'm not going down that road. That's another thing Bea and I have in common. We both hate the idea of going into the ocean. We still get our suits on, grab the lunch and drinks, and head out.

Beatrice

I absolutely love the beach. It's my favorite spot. Spending time with Chloe is the best. I never want it to end. Stupid cancer.

We lay out our blankets, sit, and have our lunch. I'm not too hungry lately, I seem to keep losing weight. I know it's the cancer, and luckily, I had some extra reserve in the weight department, but not so much anymore. Most of my clothes don't even fit anymore. Chloe has been giving me her little sister's clothes to wear. She's only ten.

After we ate, we lay back on our towels, and I quickly fell asleep. Cancer is exhausting.

I woke up to Chloe saying she'd be back and that she was going for a walk. I respond with a quick nod and drift off back to sleep. It's so warm and comfortable I think I could sleep forever. I think when I die, I hope this is how it feels.

I wake up to Chloe's voice.

"Bea. Bea. Wake up. Wake up."

"I'm awake." I sit up and grab my water, trying to make myself more awake so I can see why she's so upset.

"Did you see anyone around?" she asks.

"No," I respond. "I was sleeping and all."

"Look." She points to our beach bags. I look over and see a card on top of my bag. Someone was here. I take

the card and open the envelope. It's a plain white card inside and printed in black marker across it, it says, 'STOP LOOKING FOR ED! OR YOU WILL BE NEXT!'

I look over at Chloe. She's grabbing our stuff from the ground. She yells at me to get up. We need to get out of here before whoever left the note comes back. I agree. I can feel my heart beating fast. This must be the fight-or-flight thing I learned about at school. I can feel my heart racing. I shake and am super sweaty. This feels awful.

We grab our stuff and start walking quickly toward my house. Chloe grabs my arm and yells, "RUN!"

When someone says run, you run. You do not question it at all. We sprint across the street and run as fast as we can toward the house. I can see my house up ahead. It feels like a million miles away. I was struggling to carry my stuff while keeping up with Chloe. Chloe reaches back and grabs my hand. We pick up the pace as much as we can and make it to the front door of my house. It takes me a minute to manage to open the door. My hands are shaking too much. Finally, the door opens, we run in, and lock the door behind us. We're both out of breath. Me more than her, but still. Once I caught my breath, I asked Chloe what was that about.

"Oh my God, Bea. Did you see them? It was the Harvard guy and his fat friend. They were walking from the beach, right where we were. Harvard looked over

his shoulder at us and poked the fat one. I wasn't staying around to see what they were going to do."

"Are you serious? Do you think they followed us? Do you think they left the note?" I ask in a panicked voice.

"Seems too coincidental for them not to have left it." Chloe peeks out the window blind but says she doesn't see them out there. "What the heck do they want? Why are they threatening us with a note? They probably are following us, but why? All we've been doing is asking a few questions to see if we can find Mr. McBean. Why do they even care? We actually know nothing, just that he's missing. This can't be happening." Chloe rambles.

"Chloe, we need to talk to my dad. This has gone too far." Chloe nods in agreement. Both of us just sit with our backs against the door, afraid to move. Something's going on with Mr. McBean, and someone certainly doesn't want us to find out what.

Chloe

I have never been so scared in my life. I should never have left Bea alone. What was I thinking? If I had stayed, I would've seen if someone came around our bags. Better yet, no one would have gotten close enough to leave the note. I only went for a walk to see if I could see if Tommy was at the beach.

If he stayed at someone's house last night and slept off his hangover, he probably would have headed to the beach afterward. All this stuff going on is insane. First, Mr. McBean, then Tommy attacking Bea, and then Tommy is missing.

Now, these two crazy-looking guys coming for us. It's 4:50 PM, Bea's dad should be getting home soon. I'll feel so much better when he's home. Until then, I'm not moving.

Beatrice

We sit with our backs to the door for what seems like forever. We are both still shaking, waiting to see if the two guys show up. We're trying to be quiet, so if they do, they won't hear us and think anyone is home. Chloe puts her arm around me and whispers, "I'm sorry."

"Sorry for what? You didn't do anything wrong," I ask, surprised.

"Because I left you at the beach. If I'd stayed, we never would've gotten the note."

"Chloe, don't be silly. You are not to blame. At least now we know we're getting close to finding out what happened to Mr. McBean. We just have to be extra careful."

"Be careful? You're not thinking we should continue our search, do you? That's ridiculous. I know he's a nice person to you, but I'm done looking for him. There's no way I'm putting my life on the line for him. He's not worth it, Bea."

"He needs someone in his corner. I think we should keep looking. We just need to be careful who we talk to. Someone thinks we're getting close to finding him and doesn't want us to. Aren't you at least a little interested in finding out why?"

"Yes, but I more want to, you know, stay alive. Don't you?" Then I realized what I had just said. Of course,

Bea wants to stay alive. She just doesn't seem to have that option.

Chloe says, "I am sorry, Bea. About the staying alive part, you know what I mean. I don't think we should take any risks for him."

I reach for her hand and whisper "marshmallow."

"Chloe, let's talk to my dad and see what he thinks. Sound okay?

"You are right, Bea. Let's see what your dad has to say. He should be here in a while."

We both hear it at the same time, the door handle is turning, someone is trying to get in.

Chloe

Someone is trying to get in. We both jump up. Bea whispers we should hide and try not to make any noise. Like that is easy to do. I feel like my heart might jump out of my chest. If the two guys can get in, we don't want to be found. We crawl over to the basement stairs and quietly creep in the doorway. We both huddle on the top stair, shaking. I tell Bea that I love her, in case this goes down a bad road. Bea can't even get words out, but I know how she feels. We leave the door open a smidge so we can peek out and make sure it's them. The door handle seems stuck. We can hear the doorknob turning and not opening. I'm so glad we locked it when we ran in.

In this neighborhood, hardly anyone locks their doors. We're both so scared. Why are these two guys coming for us? All we did was ask questions about Mr. McBean. We didn't even find out anything. We still have no idea where he is or even if he is still alive.

I look over at Bea, and she doesn't look so good. She looks more afraid than me, and I feel like I may faint. This cannot be happening.

Beatrice

I'm shaking. I feel like I may pass out. The doorknob starts to turn. They're getting closer. We brace for what will happen next. I can't look. I close my eyes and wait for them to come in. I know we are not safe and they will find us. I find my voice and whisper, "I love you, besties for resties." We hold hands and both start praying.

We both scream.

Eighty pounds of chocolate lab puppy speeds over to the door and pushes it open. Peanut starts licking our faces. My dad is standing at the top of the stairs with a confused look on his face.

"What are you two up to? Why are you on the stairs? Why was the door locked?"

"Dad, you nearly gave us a heart attack. Why are you coming in the front door? You always come in by garage."

"My garage remote died. Must be dead batteries. I had to use the front door. I figured the door would be unlocked. My key was stiff in the lock. Again, what are you two doing?"

We climb up through the basement door and follow him and Peanut to the kitchen. We both are trying to catch our breath. My heart is still beating too fast. We show him the note we found on our bags, the two sketchy guys following us and thinking they were trying to break in.

He says, "Are you sure they were following you? Did you see them leave the note?"

"Well, no, not exactly."

When we go through the details, it does seem like we may have overreacted. I still think they were up to no good. My dad tells us his deputy is looking for the guys now and will let him know when they find them. He agrees the note is upsetting. He takes the note and says he'll look into it. We're both just glad he's home. He tells us to go take showers, and he'll call for a pizza delivery. Mom will be home shortly.

I turn to Chloe and say, "wow that was absolutely insane. I need a shower to get all the Peanut slobber off of me."

Chloe giggles and we head to my bedroom to get cleaned up.

Chloe

I'm so glad Bea's dad is home. I feel like a weight has been lifted. I know now we're safe. We head to Bea's room to take turns showering. Bea tells me that maybe I'm right and we shouldn't be looking into Mr. McBean so much. I'm so glad she agrees.

We decided that tonight we'll have pizza, chill here, and watch a movie. Bea looks exhausted, and I know she needs to relax and get some sleep. She has her doctor's appointment tomorrow, and I know she's eager to find out what the doctor is going to say. Bea's dad yells to us that the pizza is here. We head to the kitchen to start our relaxing night.

Beatrice

I'm so glad we are just chilling at home. The last two days have been exhausting. Mr. McBean missing, Tommy is a major jerk, and the appointment tomorrow. I just need to relax in comfy jammies, watch a mindless movie, and go to bed early. I'm so glad Chloe is all for relaxing and watching TV. She's my best friend and I love just doing nothing with her.

I can only eat one piece of pizza before my stomach decides it wants the pizza out. That's unfortunate since the pizza was delicious. I get up and get to the bathroom in the nick of time. I hate not being able to eat. The medication my mom picked up seems to help my throat, but my stomach can't handle food anymore.

I try not to let on that I am sick again and threw up my dinner, but I think everyone realizes what happened. No one seems to want to talk about it. We finish dinner and head to my room to watch a movie. I don't even know what movie we decided on, since within minutes I'm asleep.

Chloe

Bea fell asleep super quickly. That makes me happy since I know that at least she isn't thinking about her appointment tomorrow. I'm thinking about it, however. I've no idea what the doctor will say. I don't know how I'll handle it if it's worse news. We know Bea doesn't have too long, but I don't want it to be sooner than we were told. I think it must be bad news.

If it was good news, I think the doctor would have told Bea's mom on the phone. Why do bad things happen to the best people? It makes me angry with God that someone as special and beautiful as Bea has to die, and some bad people get to live.

People say, 'God only takes the special ones', or 'God must have needed someone like Bea in heaven,' and that's why she needed to die. That is bull. I don't believe it for one minute. God should take the bad eggs instead and let the good ones live.

I get up and head to the bathroom so my crying doesn't wake up Bea. She's my very best friend, and I don't want her to die. Ever.

When I get the tears to slow, I head back to Bea's bedroom. Bea is still asleep. I lie down next to her and struggle to fall asleep. Finally, sleep overtakes me.

Beatrice

I wake up, and Chloe is sitting on my side chair reading. She has already dressed for the day and smiles when she sees me wake up.

"Hey, sleepyhead. Good morning."

"What time is it? How long did I sleep? I had the weirdest dream. We were sitting with Mr. McBean on a dock, fishing. We caught a ginormous shark. It was so strange."

"That does seem strange. Somewhat cool but strange. It's nine-thirty. Your mom came up and said to wake you so you could get ready for your appointment. I was just about to get you up. Good timing."

"Thanks, Chloe. I'm going to pee and get dressed. You are coming to the appointment with me, right? Or do you want to hang out here or at the beach?"

"The beach? With the crazy Harvard guy. No, thank you. As long as your mom doesn't mind if I come, I want to go with you."

"I doubt she'll mind. She may make you stay in the car while we go inside, but then she probably will take us out to lunch. There are a lot of great restaurants near the hospital. I doubt my dad will come. He probably still is focused on Tommy."

I get dressed, grab my backpack, and we head to find my mom. Peanut is the first to greet us. Of course, with sloppy kisses. I do like having Peanut with us. If I had longer to live, I think we could get a dog. For now, we can just play with Peanut.

We head to the kitchen, and my parents are sitting at the table having coffee. Not sure why my dad isn't at work yet.

"Morning, parents of mine. What's up?"

"Just going to go up and make sure you were getting ready. We need to leave soon for the appointment."

"We're all going? Dad, don't you have to work?"

"Work can wait. I want to see what the doctor says. And besides, we found Tommy."

"You did? Where was he?" I say as I secretly hope someone beat the crap out of him.

"I talked to his mom this morning. Apparently, he waltzed in last night around midnight. He got into some fight at the bonfire and ended up crashing at his girlfriend's house. He told his mom that he was just hanging at the beach, minding his own business, and someone came over and started a fight. He fessed up and said he drank too much, and his girlfriend brought him to her house to sober up."

"Did he say who beat him up? Who is his girlfriend? I didn't even know he had one." Minding his own business? Yea right. Loser.

"He wouldn't say who beat him up. His mom asked. He just said he was going to take care of it. Whatever *that means. He must have pissed someone off and probably just doesn't remember how. His girlfriend is Angela. I don't know which one she is. Do you?"*

"We know Angela. She's basically the class tramp. I think at one time or another, she's been everyone's girlfriend, if you know what I mean."

Now I am more upset than before. Tommy doesn't know why someone beat him up. Seriously. Maybe because you tried to rape me, you piece of shit. I hate Tommy more than ever. Angela? Really? The total slut of the town. She probably loved that he was so drunk she had to take him home. I'm sure she let him do anything he wanted to her. She has a reputation for being easy.

Chloe

What a jerk Tommy is. I'm just glad he didn't mention my brother, Owen, to his mom. I would hate him to get into trouble for trying to protect Bea. Owen is such a good kid. Tommy is lucky I didn't see what he was up to with Bea. I would've killed him. I would've made sure he wouldn't attack anyone else, that's for sure.

Angela? She's a complete floozy. She has slept with so many people at school. She flirts with everyone. Always wearing slutty outfits with her boobs hanging out. She's so gross. Tommy probably slept with her and now has an STD. Serves him right. Ass.

Beatrice

We load up in the car to go to the appointment. They said it was fine for Chloe to come. They did say she probably should wait in the car. She doesn't seem to mind. She brought her next book to finish. It takes us about forty-five minutes to get to the hospital.

The hospital is known nationwide for its cancer center. Our local hospital referred me there when I was first diagnosed. It's a giant brick building with seven stories.

My doctor is located on the top floor. Always bothers me that she is on the top floor. Makes me think it is closer to heaven than the other floors. We take the elevator to the seventh floor and get sent to the waiting area while we wait for my appointment. There are seven people in the waiting area, and we all know that all of us have some kind of cancer waiting to kill us.

I try to focus on the book I brought with me, but it's hard not to look at everyone. One woman has a kid who is about two. I'm not sure which one has cancer, but either way, that sucks. Either way, you end up with a mom with no son or a son with no mom. There's a person who is like eighty. That one doesn't make me so sad. He probably had a good run. Watch. He'll probably beat cancer and live to be a hundred. Ugh.

After what seems like forever, we are finally called into Dr. Skinner's office. Dr. Skinner is my parents' age. She's really nice and told us she lost her son to a rare form of cancer when he was little. I'm not sure why she wants to be this close to cancer every day. Maybe she feels like if she can save one person, it's worth it. I just wish it were me she could save.

"Hey there, Beatrice. Good morning, Mr. and Mrs. Chase."

Not too many people I let call me Beatrice, but for someone who may be able to save my life, I let it slide.

"Good morning," my dad responds.

She asks me how I'm feeling, and I tell her about my throat hurting. I also tell her I can't eat very much. We talk about how, with this type of cancer, the symptoms I'm having are expected. She's not at all surprised by what is going on with me. My dad mentions the light bothering my eyes. She says that she hasn't heard of that before. I just stay quiet. I don't want to fess up that I had a black eye, and the glasses had nothing to do with the light.

She moves on to my recent weight loss and doesn't mention the light sensitivity again, thankfully. She takes me to the exam room for a quick exam while my parents stay in her office. I have lost another ten pounds since last month. She, again, says that is normal. She wants me to increase my protein drinks to see if I can keep them down.

We head back to her office and things get serious.

"I have called you here today to discuss Beatrice's cancer and an option going forward that you all need to contemplate. As you are all aware, the cancer Beatrice has is terminal and is progressing, as I would have expected. Beatrice seems to have lost more weight, increased mouth sores, nausea, and fatigue.

"Over time, these symptoms will get worse. That being said, there is an experimental drug available that has shown some significant results. I do not want to get your hopes up, but the medication seems to have a positive effect on patients with Beatrice's type of cancer."

My dad says, "That's great, sign her up."

"Please, let me finish. It, unfortunately, isn't as easy as that. The medication is a weekly injection. It's a pre-filled syringe and can be administered by Beatrice herself or a parent at home. Within the test patients who have taken the medication, twenty percent of them are currently cancer-free. That is astounding news.

"I say the word 'currently' cancer-free, since no one knows what the future will hold, but they are in remission today. This medication is something they will likely be on for the rest of their lives. The other eighty percent of the patients are a different story. With half of

them, the cancer progressed but did so at a slower rate. The patients in this group did pass away from their cancer, but lived longer than we expected.

"The other half had no change to their cancer trajectory and passed when we thought they would have. Of course, that's all subjective on the part of the physician. It appears to be what the data is trending. There's no guarantee that Beatrice's cancer will slow its projected path or go away completely. The data does look promising, but I certainly don't want you to think this is a sure thing."

"It seems like it is worth it to try," my dad says.

Dr. Skinner continues to talk as if she didn't hear him. "With any medication, there are side effects to consider. This medication has to be monitored closely to watch for any changes to liver and kidney function. There's also an increased risk of fertility issues as well."

My dad says, "She is sixteen. Fertility issues are the least of our problems."

"I understand. Let me continue. The biggest obstacle against this medication is the cost. The medication costs ten thousand dollars a week, for one injection. The issue is with insurance. I did confirm with your insurance policy that for the first three months of dosing, the medication would not be covered and would be your responsibility. If the insurance company sees positive

results after three months, they will cover the medication as long as she continues on it."

My mom says, "Ten thousand dollars a week? That's terrible. No one can afford that. Why even bring it up if most people can't get that much money together?"

"Hold on, maybe we can get the money together," responds my father.

"There's no way we can do that. You can't be serious." My mom retorts.

Dr. Skinner responds, "I do realize it's a lot of money, but I think you need to know all the options we have available. I reached out to the hospitals philanthropy department to see if they could help with the payment. I haven't heard yet. I will keep you posted on that.

"What I suggest you do, as a family, is go home and talk it out. Decide what you can do and what is worth doing. I know it's not an easy decision to make based on the uncertainty. Here's my home number and my direct office phone number. Call me anytime when you decide so we can move forward either way."

"That's a lot to think about. Maybe we can try to earn some money with a fundraiser, or we could take another mortgage on the house. We need to see what we can pull together. It seems like it is worth a chance. Thanks for the information. We will be in touch in the next day or two," my dad answers.

"Sounds good. Take care. Beatrice, if you have any more discomfort, please call me anytime, day, or night."

"Thanks, Dr. Skinner."

Chloe

Finally, they're done. That seemed to take forever. I thought I was going to die from starvation waiting that long. They're walking across the parking lot, but something seems off. No one is talking. They're just walking along, and all seem upset. This can't be good. I was hoping they would've gotten some good news, not bad. Poor Bea. I kind of wish I had stayed home. This will not be a good ride back, seems like it may be sad.

"Hi Bea. Are you okay? What happened?"

It looks like she is about to cry. Her eyes are tearing up. She seems so upset. She finally whispers, "I don't want to talk about it. I just want to go home. Is that okay, marshmallow?"

"Of course, Bea. I'm always here for you. Whenever you want to talk. Besties for the resties." I reach over and hold her hand. It doesn't feel like enough, but for now, it is all I can do.

Her dad and mom also aren't talking, so the car ride is a tad bit awkward. We head straight home, which is disappointing since I was hoping for a nice lunch in the city. Damn cancer.

Beatrice

Well, that sucked.

There's no way we can afford that much money. My mom is constantly clipping coupons to save money. She complains all the time about being broke and wishing she was well off. Although we probably wouldn't be broke if she didn't spend all their money on skin products, hair and nail appointments, and clothes. I would love to start the injections and see what happens.

I feel like I have nothing to lose and only living to gain. I don't think anyone could afford ten thousand a week. Three months' worth would be a hundred and twenty thousand dollars. Our house didn't even cost that much. We drive straight home and no one talks at all. I know my mom and dad are spending the ride thinking about how to make it work. I don't see how it can.

We pull into the driveway and get out of the car. My dad says he's going to head to the station. My mom says they need to talk, privately, before he leaves, that can't be good.

We go inside, and they head for the basement to talk. I grab Chloe's hand and pull her over toward the vent on the floor over the basement area. Not sure why it is, but we can hear everything they say from this spot. I whisper to Chloe to be quiet and listen and that I'll explain everything later.

My parents are arguing, which, luckily for me, makes it easier to hear what they have to say. My mom is adamant that we can't come up with the money, and it's breaking her heart. My dad keeps saying he'll figure something out. He says that maybe they could afford it if she didn't get her nails and hair done all the time. I kind of agree with him. She spends a lot on herself. Like all the time.

My mom brings up again that maybe they can take out another mortgage on the house. My dad says they already took out another mortgage to pay for my medical bills. He says the house isn't worth it and that the bank will never give them more money. I hear my dad say something about asking his dad. He says his dad might be able to help. My mom says she will not ask him and can't believe he even mentioned it.

As far as I know, they haven't spoken to my grandfather for years. He never liked my mom and didn't think my dad should be with her. They had a falling out before I was even born. I have never met him. They decide to talk about things later and let it sink in. I hear them coming up the stairs. I grab Chloe and head to my room before they see us.

We get to my room, and I close the door. I sit down and tell Chloe everything that the doctor told us. I tell her about the side effects and the percentage of people that it actually helps. I tell her about the cost and that I know we can't afford it. She starts to cry. She hugs me and tells me it'll be alright. I know she has no way of knowing that it will be alright, but I agree anyway.

Chloe

How can it be that expensive to help someone? I know there's no way they can afford it. I wish I could help, but I have like twenty dollars to my name. I can ask my parents, but I don't think they have it either. My mom doesn't even work. I told Bea that everything would be okay, but I don't really think it will.

Beatrice

By the time we head out to the kitchen, both of my parents have left. My dad went to work and my mom went off to show a house. We pack a lunch and walk down to the beach. It's such a nice day today, the beach is busy. We spend a few hours chatting, relaxing, and watching the waves when Chloe says, "Look, there's Tommy."

I look over, and sure enough, there he is with Angela. They are sitting close together on one towel with his arms around her back. Gross. If only she knew what a slime bag he was. I'm sure she has no idea. I would tell her, but she deserves him as much as he deserves her.

"Let's just leave," I say as I start to turn and walk away.

"Oh crap, Bea, he's heading over."

Sure enough, here comes Tommy. Oddly, Angela stayed at the towel. I really can't deal with this today. I try not to look at him, hoping he's just walking by, but no. Here is he.

"Hey, Bea. Hey, Chloe. Nice day, huh?"

"What the hell do you want, Tommy? We want nothing to do with you," responds Chloe.

"Why not? Bea seemed like she wanted me the other night. She was hot and heavy. If it weren't for your

stupid brother, she would've had a good time. Would've made her whole short life seem worth it."

Chloe jumped up and went over to him. She slapped him in the face. I just sat there, crying. Why is he such a jerk? What did I ever do to him?

Tommy grabbed Chloe's hand after she slapped him and pulled her toward him.

Tommy says, "Hold up there, sunshine. What the hell was that about? Maybe it would have been more fun to be with you at the party? You are feisty. Not sure why you are so mad, I'm only stating facts. I came over to tell you that if I ever see your brother again, I will kill him. You make sure you tell him that. He best not show up anywhere near me again. Next time he comes near me, you'll be visiting him in the morgue."

"Piss off," Chloe yells, as she pulls her arm away. "I have no problem going to the police and letting them in on what you tried to do to Bea. If you ever touch my brother, me, or Bea again, so help me God, I'll go to the cops. I'm sure Bea's dad would love to hear what you did to her. I doubt he'd let you off easy."

"You won't go to the cops. Her daddy can't do anything since she wanted it to happen."

"No one wants that to happen. Maybe your sleaze of a girlfriend, but other than that, no one. Get the heck away from us. Actually, maybe your girlfriend would

like me to let her know what happened. I think I'll call her over and have a nice chat." Chloe responds.

"Stay away from my girlfriend. You two are just two crazy bitches. Not even worth my time."

At that, Tommy turns and heads back to Angela.

As he walks away, Chloe yells, "Hey, Angela. Ask your loser boyfriend what happened at the bonfire. You may be interested to know what kind of guy you're dating."

Tommy grabs Angela's arm and walks off the beach toward the street.

Good riddance.

Chloe

I am so mad right now. Who does Tommy think he is? I hate him so much for what he did to Bea. If he thinks he'll get near my brother, he has another thing coming. I do hope I can talk to Angela and make sure she knows what he is. Total jerk.

I look over, and Bea is crying. I feel so bad for her right now. I go over, sit next to her, and put my arm around her.

"It'll be okay, Bea, promise. Karma will get him."

"Thanks, Chloe."

I tell Bea that I had enough of the beach today, even though we just got there and that we should go to Sunnys and grab a shake. She agrees, and we grab our stuff and head out.

Beatrice

We get to the diner, and Lenny is standing outside smoking. I swear that every time we come here, he's there. I whisper to Chloe, "No wonder it seems like cars are always being worked on at his shop. It's probably just one car he hasn't finished yet." We both start to laugh. I'm feeling better already.

"Hey, Lenny. What's up?"

"Nothing with me. Busy working." Chloe and I look at each other and try to hold in our laugh.

"Did you find anything else about Mr. McBean?" Chloe asks.

"Nope. Still radio silence."

"Lenny, do you know if Mr. McBean still has his fishing cabin?"

"His fishing cabin? No. He sold it a few years back. Some young couple bought it, tore it down, and built a bigger cabin. From what I hear, it's super nice. They spend a lot of time there. They're residents of New York. Why are you asking about his old cabin?"

"Just wondering. Someone mentioned it to us, and we weren't sure if it was still there?"

"Nope, not there anymore."

"Have you seen your friend, Mike? The guy you go to breakfast with. Wondering if he's heard from Mr. McBean?"

"Mike? Sure, I see Mike. Just saw him yesterday. We met up for lunch. He hasn't seen Ed either. He said he thinks Ed headed out of town for vacation."

"Really? Seems weird he'd leave Peanut?" Chloe says.

"Not sure. I agree with Mike and we should just leave Ed be. He'll come back when he's good and ready. Well, I have to get back to work. Take care, girls."

Chloe

That was strange. We sit on the curb and talk it over. Bea agrees it was strange. The story about the fishing cabin? Seems wrong. If someone bought and built a cabin, surely people around town would know about it. Especially Bea's dad. The part about Mike thinking he's on vacation, again, seems wrong. Mr. McBean would never leave Peanut and go off on a vacation, especially without letting Bea know so she could watch Peanut. Maybe Bea's dad has some information on Mike or the cabin.

We go into the diner and immediately see Vic behind the counter.

"Hey there, girls. How are you two doing today? Two shakes for you?"

"Yes, please. We're good. Just wanted to get out of the sun and cool off."

"I am glad you're here. A few people have been asking about you. They're sitting over in the corner. Head on over, and I will grab your drinks."

Beatrice

We head over to the last booth in the corner and find the two sketchy guys sitting there. We turn to leave. Vic moves us closer to them and asks us what's the matter?

"Where are you guys heading? These two nice people have been waiting for some time. Here are your shakes. Let me grab you some pie. I have one that just came out of the oven."

We hesitantly sit down. I'm sitting next to Harvard guy, and Chloe is next to the chubby one. Probably would've been smarter to change seats since I am a lot thinner than Chloe, and chubby guy seems to take up most of the bench seat. We stay where we are.

Harvard guy says, "We're hoping you would show up. We know you guys are still asking around for Ed, and we think maybe you need to stop. It'd be in your best interest to let sleeping dogs lie."

"Why are you so interested in what we're doing? We don't even know who you are. And after you left us that threatening note, we want nothing to do with you," Chloe says.

"Note? What note?"

"The note you left on our swim bags. Telling us to stop looking for Mr. McBean and threatening to hurt us. Sound familiar? We saw you leaving the beach right after we found it."

"Who said we left the note? We don't even know what you're talking about. We're just two concerned citizens who feel you should stop wasting your time looking for Ed. At the beach, we saw you two and wanted to tell you that, but you guys bolted, and we couldn't see where you went," the chubby guy responds.

"So, who are you? And why do you care if we look for Mr. McBean?"

"It's not important who we are and why we want you to stop. The truth is, we think he needs to be left alone. We are only thinking of him."

Chloe says, "That makes zero sense. We've never even seen you two around here until Mr. McBean went missing. Who knows what you guys might have done to him? As of two minutes ago, we thought you left the mean note. We are still not convinced you didn't leave the note."

"Well, we didn't. In the best interest of Mr. McBean and for your safety, it seems to make sense to leave things be."

I give Chloe the eyes that tell her we should leave. We get up at the same time. Chubby guy grabs Chloe's arm and says, "Think about it. It'd be in your best interest not to go against us, if you know what I mean?"

He lets go of Chloe's arm, and we rush toward the door. I turn to Vic and say, "Those two are picking up the tab for the shakes. Thanks, Vic." We leave.

Chloe

Once we're outside, we both start to breathe again. That was super scary. Who do they think they are? We still don't know their names or what they're up to. I still think they left the note to scare us. Bea agrees. We talk as we walk toward her house.

We look back a few times to make sure no one is following us. So far, so good. We both decide we need to talk to Bea's dad and find out more information. We get to Bea's house, head to her room, and turn on the television while we wait for her parents to get home.

We're watching *Days of Our Lives* while we finish our shakes. Both of us are tired from the day. First, the cancer doctor's appointment, then Tommy, then the two crazy guys. We both are too tired to even talk to each other. That's a sign that we're the best of friends.

Besties for the resties.

Beatrice

Right in the middle of Hope kissing Bo, again, a breaking news alert came on the TV.

BREAKING NEWS UPDATE

We have breaking news that just came into the station. A body has been discovered. Two local kids discovered the body of an older white male while fishing at Hemlock Lake. The youths called 911 after seeing a body floating in the water on the north side of the lake. The victim's identity has not yet been identified, according to officials at the scene. As of now, the facts of the case are still unclear. Chief Chase is at the scene and has given the following statement.

"At approximately 3 PM today, two local teens fishing at the edge of Hemlock Lake saw a body floating in the lake. The young men called 911. Upon arrival, the body of an older white male was removed from the water. Divers are on scene to look for any remaining evidence in the water. This is an open investigation due to evidence found at the scene of foul play. The victim's name will not be made public at this time due to pending notification to the family. Thank you."

"Thank you, Chief Chase. The chief has asked the public to stay away from the area at this time. As we get more details into the station, we will update the public. According to reports, it appears that the body has been in the water for a few days. The medical examiner is on the scene. To recap, the body of an older man was found dead and has yet to be identified. It appears to be suspicious in nature."

This is Michelle Young, News Channel One

The breaking news alert ends, and Hope and Bo are still kissing. Chloe and I are just staring at the TV. Both of us are speechless. Could it be Mr. McBean? Maybe?

Chloe

"Bea, I can't believe it. It must be Mr. McBean?"

"I don't understand. How can he be dead? Who would've done this to him? He was such a nice person. He never bothered anyone. I can't believe it."

"Me either. Mr. McBean is dead. And they think he was killed? Who would've done that to him?"

"I don't know, Chloe. I just don't know."

"Do you think it was the Harvard guy?" Chloe asks.

"Maybe? I mean, we were with them today, and they seemed to be adamant we leave Mr. McBean alone. Maybe they killed him and wanted to make sure no one found him. Guess it's too late for that. I keep thinking of the two prisoners. They were supposed to be heading our way, and they're still on the run. Do you think maybe they found Mr. McBean while trying to locate the missing money and killed him?"

Chloe responds, "Maybe. It'd make sense. They're not good people, and I'm sure they'd like to get their hands on the money. Why kill him? Unless they ended up finding the money and didn't want to split it with him or the fourth guy, Mike."

"Maybe. It just doesn't seem to add up. I think if I were Mike and was the fourth person, I'd be scared that I would be next. That's if they didn't get the money information from Mr. McBean. I just don't know."

"What about Kyle? He hated Rachel's dad, and they did just have a fight. Maybe he found him and decided he wanted him gone," Chloe says.

"It could've been him. They certainly didn't like each other. Kyle seems like a loose cannon. I think if it was the Harvard pair, the prisoners, or Kyle, all of them didn't seem like the brightest bulbs in the circuit. They must have left some type of evidence behind. If anyone is going to solve this, it'll definitely be my dad."

"True. What should we do?"

Beatrice

We decided we should write a list of what we know and need to find out about Mr. McBean to give to my dad to help with the case.

Who killed Mr. McBean?
1. *Prisoners*
    a. *They may be in the area.*
    b. *Mad, they didn't have all the money. Need money since they're on the run.*
    c. *Motive - Don't want to go back to prison. Need cash to keep running.*
2. *Harvard guy and chubby friend*
    a. *Very interested in Mr. McBean.*
    b. *Won't tell us who they are or what they want.*
    c. *Seem to be trying to get us out of the picture.*
    d. *Don't seem too bright.*
    e. *Motive?*
3. *Kyle*
    a. *Angry and hates Mr. McBean.*
    b. *Knows the area around Hemlock Lake.*
    c. *Motive—Revenge on getting beat up.*
4. *Mike*
    a. *The fourth guy?*

  b. Does he have the money?

  c. Is he next?

5. Lenny

  a. Lied about the lighter.

  b. Lied about seeing the two sketchy guys at his job.

  c. Motive? Money?

6. Carl (Mr. McBean's mom's friend at the nursing home)

  a. Mentioned fishing cabin.

  b. Does Mr. McBean still have the fishing cabin? How far is the cabin from where Mr. McBean was found?

  c. No way could he be involved. Too old and stuck in the nursing home.

  d. No motive.

We have no idea when my dad will be home, so we decide to head to Chloe's house and eat there. Her mom is making spaghetti and meatballs, and that's both our favorite meal. Maybe Owen will be there. Fingers crossed.

Chloe

I'm so glad to be going home tonight, even if it's only for dinner. I just want to get away from Mr. McBean after being found dead, just for a little while. I think he's a nice person, but he sure seems to have some issues with people. It actually isn't that much of a shock to me that someone killed him. He probably deserved it after he ratted out his friends and beat up Kyle. His own daughter doesn't even like him.

If it weren't for Bea, I wouldn't be interested in finding him. I know it's important to Bea. Maybe because it's taking her mind off of her dying. I'm going to miss my best friend. I wish I had the money to save her.

On our way to my house, we walk over and find Bea's mom in the living room with the TV on.

Beatrice

"Hi, Mom."

"Hey, girls. Did you see the breaking news alert?"

"We did. Seems scary that something happened this close to home. Did they give any updates on who it is? Did they confirm it's Mr. McBean?" I respond.

"Nothing yet. I'm sure your dad will be home late, maybe not even until tomorrow. I was thinking the same thing about Mr. McBean. He was a nice man and certainly didn't deserve to die at the hands of someone else."

"Mom, I don't think anyone deserves that."

"You're right, of course. I just hope he's in a better place now. It's God's will, after all. Once they confirm it's him and let Rachel know, I'm going to bring her over a casserole. I want to let her know I'm available to sell his house. I think I can get a lot for it."

"Mom, why do you always do that? The man just died. He was my friend, and all you can think about is selling his house for a profit. I can't believe you."

"I'm sorry you feel that way. The truth of the matter is he's dead, and someone has to sell his house. Why not me? We can use the money to help pay for your injections."

I respond, "I don't even think I want the injections. Now that Mr. McBean is gone. Especially not using his *money. Mom, thinking about selling his house, is just cold. I can't believe you think it's a good thing. We're heading over to Chloe's for dinner. See ya."*

"Bea, don't be like that. I'm only trying to figure out how we can get the money to help you get better. It's not like I killed the man."

Beatrice

I can't believe my mom is acting that way. It isn't always about money. Someone who I really cared for is dead, and all she can think about is selling his house and making money. Probably so she can get more face cream.

I'm not even sure I want the experimental drug injections. There's only a slight chance of it curing me. Adding more time to feel sick longer seems stupid. I think God has a plan, and I want Him to decide what happens, not me or my mother.

Being best friends with Chloe sometimes means we don't even have to talk for her to know what I'm feeling. As we walk to her house, she puts her arm around me, and we just walk in silence.

We go into her house, and her mom is cooking dinner. It smells heavenly. My mom pretty much tries to eat healthy, and I've had my fill of salads. I think she thinks if I eat too many carbs, the cancer will never go away. I may never want to go home.

Chloe

"Hi, Mom,"

"Well, there you are. Nice of you to show your face around here. I knew I had a daughter around here somewhere, she just never seems to want to come home. All this time, all it took was me making meatballs and spaghetti. I may have to make it every day from now on just so I can see your beautiful face."

"Hi, Mrs. Carpenter," Bea says.

"Well, hello there, Bea. Happy to see you. How are you feeling?"

Bea tilts her head to the side like she's not too sure how she feels, but responds, "Doing good. One day at a time." Sometimes it is just easier for her to say all is good than to continue the conversation.

We sit at the table with her, talking while dinner is being cooked. We talk about the experimental injections. We talk about Mr. McBean and the breaking news. She didn't know anything, since she doesn't really watch TV. She mostly reads books.

We talk about the beach, the start of school, and how Bea probably won't be able to go. She's a great mom. We only spend all our time at Bea's house because her mom doesn't care what we do, and my mom is a tad over-protective. My mom is a much better listener, that's for sure. Bea looks more relaxed than I have seen her in a long time.

Beatrice

Just sitting at Chloe's kitchen table feels like a weight has been lifted off me. Her mom is the best. Every time I say something, it's as if I am the only important thing in her life. I know I'm not, but it's just how she makes me feel. I wish she were my mom.

We sit and talk about everything. We update her on Mr. McBean and everyone who we think could be responsible. She agrees with us on all counts. She was surprised he was killed. She tells us she doesn't know very much about him. That he was a quiet neighbor who didn't seem to bother anyone.

We talked about the experimental injections. She says she'll talk to Chloe's dad to see if they'd be able to help. She wasn't sure how much she could help, but would see what they could do. Much different from my mom quickly saying it was too much money, that speaks volumes.

We set the table for dinner, and in comes Owen. He's so cute. I walk over to him and give him a hug. I thank him for helping me at the bonfire. I can't say too much because Chloe's mom has no idea we even went to the bonfire. Owen gives me a hug back. It seems like the hug lasts a bit longer than it needs to, maybe that's just my imagination playing tricks on me. Wishful thinking. It just feels so right. My hero.

Chloe

Well, that was weird. Seeing Bea and Owen hug. Not a bad sort of weird, more like a good sort of weird. I think Bea really likes my brother, and from that hug, I think he may feel the same. I would've liked to see them get together. With Bea dying and all, I'm hoping they don't. I don't want to see my brother get hurt.

Once they stop hugging, we head to the kitchen for dinner. The meal is great, and I like being at home. Seems like most of the time, we hang out at Bea's house. Maybe we should start spending more time at mine. It seems like there's so much more love here compared to her house.

As we sit and eat dinner, we chat about what Owen has been up to. The conversation is light. We don't talk about Mr. McBean at all. It's refreshing. We laugh at the stories Owen tells us about some people who go into Walmart. He works in the pharmacy department. He'd like to go to college to become a pharmacist. He's been working there part time for the past year.

He tells us about a guy coming in last week telling the pharmacist that the medication his doctor prescribed wasn't working. The pharmacist asked him how often he was using them. The guy said he was taking them every four hours. The pharmacist asked how exactly he had been taking them and that every four hours was too much. The guy said he took the pills with water every four hours for the past few days, and he's still constipated. He feels like the pills aren't working.

The pharmacist explained to the guy that the medication was not pills. They were suppositories. He explained they were supposed to be put in the guy's butt and not swallowed. We are laughing so hard that Bea actually spits out some of her pasta. It was hilarious.

The guy was swallowing the things he was supposed to put in his butt and didn't understand why they weren't working. The poor guy. No wonder he's still constipated. We spend the rest of dinner just laughing at the poor guy.

After dinner, we pick up the table and clean the kitchen. We look out the window, and Bea's dad's car isn't in the driveway, so we decide to stay at my house tonight. We end up sitting on the living room couch, watching television and having popcorn. Owen stays with us. It's such a nice, relaxing night with no drama. At one point, it looked like Bea and Owen were holding hands under the blanket.

Beatrice

Tonight has been the best night of the Summer of C. First, the hug from Owen, and then he grabbed my hand under the blanket while we were watching TV. He just held my hand. It was the sweetest thing ever. I like him so much. I can't wait to tell Chloe after he leaves to go to sleep. I hope she's happy about it. I know I am.

We all end up falling asleep watching television. I wake up when I feel Owen getting up. He looks at me and kisses my forehead. He whispers, "Don't tell Chloe yet."

I nod okay, and he says he will talk to me later. Owen kissed my forehead. I think he really likes me. That's all I ever wanted. I want to tell Chloe, but I told Owen I'd wait. I'll try my best to wait. It feels like torture.

Chloe gets up a little while later and looks at me weirdly. As if she knows something is up.

I say, "Why are you looking at me funny?"

She says, "You look guilty. Did you do something?"

"No. I didn't do anything. Stop looking at me weird."

"Did you hold my brother's hand under the blanket last night?"

"No. What's wrong with you? Why would you even say that?"

"Sorry, Bea. I must've had a bizarre dream. Let's get ready for the day and grab something to eat. Maybe your dad is home, and we can see what he knows."

"Sounds good. Just don't give me that weird look again. It's freaking me out."

"You got it," Chloe says.

I hated not to tell Chloe about me and Owen. As soon as he gives me the green light, I will rush to tell her. I am not surprised she thinks something is up, since we are besties and all. Sometimes I think we can read each other's mind. It's like we can communicate without even talking out loud.

Chloe

I know something is up with her and Owen. I know what I saw. They were totally holding hands. I saw him kiss her forehead. They thought I was still sleeping, but I wasn't. I saw the whole thing. I'm not sure if I'm happy about it or not.

I mean, I'm happy for Bea. I know she really likes my brother. I know she doesn't have much time left, so it would be nice for her to have a boyfriend before she dies.

But Owen? I don't want him to get hurt when he loses Bea. For now, I think I'll let them think I'm clueless. I know Bea will tell me when she's ready, and it'll give me a chance to figure out what I will say. Bea and Owen? They actually make a super cute couple.

Beatrice

I think Chloe thinks something is going on between Owen and me. For now, I will pretend she doesn't know, so we don't have to talk about it. I tried my best to sound convincing that nothing was going on, but I don't think she fell for it. Once I talk to Owen, we can decide what to tell her.

We get dressed and head over to my house. My dad's car is in the driveway. Maybe he can tell us more about Mr. McBean.

When we go in, my mom is sitting at the kitchen counter having a cup of coffee. She asks about our night and seems oblivious that I was mad at her last night. All she thinks about is herself and earning more money. Poor Mr. McBean dies and all my mother can think about is selling his house for the commission.

"Hey, girls. Have fun last night?"

"Yeah, it was fun. We watched TV, ate too much popcorn, and laughed a lot. What time did Dad get home?"

"Just a little bit ago. He was at the crime scene most of the night and slept at the station. He wants to talk to you two, so don't go too far."

"Okay. We'll be in my room."

We head to my bedroom, sit awkwardly, and wait. I want to tell her about Owen, but I know I shouldn't. I think with a friendship like ours, we don't have to say anything to hear what the other is saying. We sit quietly and listen to music while we wait for my dad.

Chloe

I want to tell her I know about her and my brother. I wish she'd just tell me already. I think she needs to start the conversation. I don't want to sound like I'm against it, even though I may be.

We sit and listen to music. It seems to take forever for her dad to come to see us. In reality, it wasn't too long, but when there's an elephant in the room you want to talk about but won't, it seems a lot longer.

"Hey, girls. I wanted to talk to you before I head back to the station. I know you watched the news last night and saw what went on at Hemlock Lake. I know what everyone thinks has happened, and I wanted you to hear it from me first. I have a press conference in an hour to let the public know, but felt you should hear it from me first."

"Thanks, Dad. We feel so bad for Mr. McBean. He didn't deserve to die. He was such a great person, and no matter what he got into, I think he changed. No one should be killed, but of all people, not Mr. McBean. It makes me sad," Bea says with a tear running down her cheek. I reach over and give her a hug, whispering marshmallow.

Bea's dad says, "Bea and Chloe, it's true that a man was found murdered. He was in the lake for a few days at least. The medical examiner confirms he died between thirty-six and forty-eight hours ago. He had been beaten up pretty bad. Because of the trauma to his face as well as the condition of the body being in the water for some time. We were unable to identify him by looking at him.

"The victim also had two gunshot wounds that were found upon the medical examiner's preliminary examination. One to the chest and one to the head. It is being ruled a homicide. He was dead before being thrown into the lake. We used fingerprints, as well as dental records, to identify the body. It was confirmed it was not Mr. McBean."

Beatrice

"What? It wasn't Mr. McBean? How's that possible? I can't believe it. That's such a relief. Who was it? Is it someone we know?"

"The victim was identified as Michael Keller. His wife came in today and made a positive ID. Mike was Mr. McBean's friend. He was the person who met up with Ed and Lenny at the diner. He worked at the mill with Mr. McBean."

"Mike? Mike, the person who was maybe the fourth man in the fraud scheme? That Mike?"

"One and the same. Right now, our only lead is with the escaped prisoners. They were seen in the area a few days ago. They're still on the run. We've called the FBI to help with the investigation. I wanted you to hear from me it wasn't Mr. McBean. We still have no leads as to where he is. I still have men on the lookout for him. We talked to the two guys you said were asking for him, but they don't seem to be involved. Their story of why they are in town seems plausible. For now, they're not off my radar, but don't seem to be my guys."

"I'm shocked it wasn't Mr. McBean. I was so sure that Mr. McBean was the person who was killed. Why Mike? It must all come back to the missing money," Chloe says.

"That's what we're thinking. We're not sure yet who's behind it, but it certainly seems like it has to do with the

fraud case. With all the signs leading to Mike as the fourth person involved, it seems likely that it has something to do with the missing money."

"What about Lenny? When we talked to him, he clearly had been lying about a few things?"

"We talked to Lenny. He seemed shocked that Mike was dead. He was emotional. I just don't see him being involved. That being said, everyone is still on my radar. Although Lenny does seem harmless."

"Then why did he lie?" I ask.

Chloe

Mike? It was Mike. That's unbelievable. We for sure thought it was going to be Mr. McBean. Why would someone hurt Mike? Clearly, it has to do with the fraud scheme and the missing money. I'm more and more confused about what's going on.

"Do you think Mr. McBean is in real trouble? If someone killed Mike to get information, the next logical person to get information out of would be Mr. McBean. That's if someone hasn't already killed him, too."

Bea's dad says, "That's exactly right. I have all my staff on the lookout for Mr. McBean. I just hope that we find him before someone else does. I fear he may be next."

Beatrice

We show my dad our list of information about Mr. McBean. My dad seems to think we did a good job. He takes the list we made and says he's going to look into it. Before he gets up to leave for the station, he tells us to stay safe. He suggests we take a break from looking for Mr. McBean, since it may be dangerous at this time to be involved. I think he's right.

"Bea. I wanted to let you know I called your grandfather, my dad. I wanted to ask him about lending me some money for your injections. He wants to meet you. What do you think about that?"

"Does he know about me at all? I never heard you talk about him very much. I knew Mom's dad died when I was young, but you never talked about your family."

"I'm sorry about that. Your mom's dad died shortly after you were born of a heart attack. My dad never approved of me being with your mom, and we had a falling out. This was before I married your mom. I haven't talked to him in the last eighteen years. He had no idea he had a granddaughter. I called out of desperation for you. You mean the world to me, Bea, and I'm hoping he can help. I'm sorry that I never gave you the chance to meet him before now. I'm truly sorry about that and hope you can forgive me."

"I forgive you, Dad. I'm not sure I want to try the injections. I haven't really even decided if that's something I want."

"I think it's time for you to meet your grandfather either way. It's been too long. I shouldn't have decided for you not to know him because of my feelings toward him. Will you agree to meet him? He wants to meet you today?"

"I will, Dad. However, I want to meet him because he's my grandpa, not meet him because he may have money to give me. Deal?"

"Deal. I need to go to the station for a bit and file a report. I also have to hold a press conference. I'll be back after lunch to pick you up. And just so you know, your mom is not too happy about you meeting him. But let me handle that. Chloe, you're invited to come with us to see Bea's grandfather."

"Thanks, Dad."

"Thanks, Mr. Chase."

My dad closes the bedroom door and heads out. Today's going to be interesting. I'm going to meet my grandfather. I don't even know what to say to one. I have a ton of questions about how to talk to one. Good thing Chloe's here, she has two grandfathers. Luckily, she can tell me what to say to one.

Chloe

Bea has a grandfather that she never met. I'd hate not knowing my grandpas. Mine are both very sweet and mean the world to me. Her grandfather didn't even know she was born. I wonder how this meeting is going to go. I love Bea, but sometimes she can be a lot to handle. I hope he's everything to her. I think Bea could use something positive in her life right now.

I decide I am going to stay home. I think this is something she needs to do alone. I know she won't like me staying home while she goes off to meet him, but she needs to be 100% in and not worried about me. I just hope it goes well.

"Bea, I think, if you don't mind, I'm going to stay home while you go to see your grandpa. I have a headache and just want to lie down in my own bed. Please don't be mad. As soon as you come home, I'll be right over. Promise."

Bea responds, "That's okay, Chloe. You don't have to go. I kind of think this is something I have to do alone, anyway. I just hope he likes me and isn't disappointed in who I am."

"Bea, that's ridiculous. You're beautiful inside and out, and I am sure he'll see that when he meets you."

Beatrice

My dad pulls up to the house around 1:30, and I walk out to his car. I'm terrified about meeting my grandfather. He did not know until today that I even existed. This isn't going to be easy.

My dad asks where Chloe is, and I tell him she has a headache. I don't think she really is sick. I think she just said that so she wouldn't have to go with me. I can understand that, and in a way, I think this is something I need to do alone. I don't care about his money and hope he says he won't give it to me.

It'd be a much easier decision about the injections if I didn't have a decision to make. All I know about him is that his name is Charles. My grandmother died years ago, and my grandpa has lived alone with his two dogs. That seems sad. I hope I don't let him down once he sees who I am. His one son only has one kid, and she's broken. That has to be hard to handle. So much for leaving a legacy.

It doesn't take us too long to get to his house, about an hour ride. He lives in a cute cape-style house with a white picket fence around the property. When we pull up, my dad says that the house looks the same as it did when he last saw it. Eighteen years ago. I'm not sure who's more nervous, me, or my dad.

We climb out of the car and head up the walk. Two adorable small white terriers greet us. They're so cute and friendly. I sit right down, and they climb all over me. They can't stop licking me. I am in heaven.

The front door opens, and standing there is a man who eerily looks like an older version of my dad, except he has really gray hair and a mean look in his eyes. Maybe this is a bad idea. I look at my dad, and he nudges me forward toward the door.

When I get close, my grandpa gruffly says, "So, I take it this is the granddaughter that I didn't even realize I had?"

My dad says, "I would like to introduce you to your granddaughter, Beatrice."

I chime in, "My friends call me Bea."

My grandpa does not look very happy. He looks annoyed that we are here. He says, "Well, Beatrice, you might as well come in and get this over with."

I knew this would not go well. I should never have agreed to come.

"It'll be okay Bea. Let's go in and get to know your grandpa."

We walk up the few steps to the door when my grandpa says, "No need for you to stay. This is between Beatrice and me. She'll call when we're through for a ride home."

I'm sure my dad wasn't expecting that. He didn't know what to do. I am slightly terrified but manage to say, "It'll be okay, Dad. I'll call when I'm ready to come home. I'd like to stay and get to know my grandfather."

I don't really mean it, but it would be weird to say that I already don't like him.

I think I need to be brave. I know if Chloe were here with me, she would tell me I can do it.

"Are you sure, Bea?"

"I'm sure. Thanks, Dad. I'll call when I'm done."

I head inside with a strange man who already doesn't seem to like me.

The house is actually very neat and clean. I don't know why I assumed it would be messy. The dogs are in the house with us, so I ask him what their names are to kind of break the ice. He says one is Muffin and the other one is Bagel. I start to laugh at their names. My grandfather looks offended. I tell him the names are cute, but not what I would've expected an old person to name his two dogs. He doesn't seem to see that as funny. Great, now he has one more reason not to like me.

He asks if I would like to sit down and get to know each other. I sit on the floor so I can play with the dogs while we talk. We spend a few minutes talking about his dogs, which seems to make him a smidge happy.

When we run out of things to say, I ask him about what my dad was like when he was young. I can see that was a good thing to ask since my grandpa started telling me stories about my dad when he was young. I can tell from how he talks that he really does care for my dad.

I tell him some stories of growing up with his son being my dad, and we both end up laughing. Sharing stories at my dad's expense seems to have opened up my grandpa's heart.

We talk about my mom. He said he wants to get together with her and apologize for how he behaved. I told him she was high maintenance, and he just laughed and said he wasn't surprised.

I tell him about my best friend, Chloe. I tell him about how we're besties for the resties. He told me that his wife, my dad's mom, was his best friend. He also tells me that I look like her when she was young. He says she was the most beautiful woman in the world.

He asks me questions about my cancer diagnosis. I tell him everything. Maybe it's because I lost sixteen years with him, and I'm trying to make sure he knows it all so he doesn't feel like he missed out on anything.

We talk about the injections that everyone except me thinks are a good thing. He asks me why I don't want to get them. I tell him I'm afraid they won't work and I'll get my hopes up for nothing. I also tell him I haven't felt well in a long time, and if the injections make me live longer feeling sick, that wouldn't be fun at all.

I tell him maybe me dying is what God has planned for me. He says that sometimes you have to take a chance and hope things will work out. I tell him I don't know if I'm brave enough for that. He tells me that any granddaughter of his has bravery in her blood, just as he does.

We end up playing cards at his kitchen table, and he makes me a grilled cheese sandwich for dinner. I win almost every game we play. He might've let me win a few. I didn't deserve to win, but I didn't let on that I knew he let me win.

We watched a movie after dinner and kept on talking. I really like him. He seems to like me, too. At least he's smiling now and not so grumpy. He says that he was sorry we had never met before. He says he made mistakes in his past with his son that he never should have made. I tell him it isn't too late to make amends. He says he hoped it wasn't. I think I saw him cry a little.

It was about 9:00 when he says I guess you should call your dad and get on home. I asked if it would be okay if I stayed. I don't want to leave him now that he is part of my life. He says I can stay as long as my dad says it's okay.

He tells me to ask my dad to come back and pick me up in the morning. He wants me to tell my dad he needs to talk to him. I called, and my dad said it was fine for me to stay and that he'd be over around 9:00 in the morning to pick me up. I called Chloe and told her I'd talk to her tomorrow. I didn't want her to worry.

In the morning, my grandpa makes me pancakes for breakfast while we wait for my dad to show up. My dad pulls up right around 9:00 with Chloe. I'm so happy Chloe came. I can't wait for her to meet my grandpa and his two adorable pups.

My grandpa asked me if Chloe and I would take the dogs for a walk so he could speak privately to my dad. How could we say no to such cute, happy puppies?

Chloe

I missed Bea so much. It seemed like we were apart forever, and it was only one night. I don't know how I will survive without her. We put the leashes on the dogs and head out. Her grandfather lives in a small neighborhood that's great for walking the dogs. It's like a big circle.

We start walking, and Bea tells me about her night. She tells me some stories about her dad that her grandpa told her. She tells me about how she told him all about her mom and growing up. She said she told him about her cancer. She said they played cards and watched movies. She tells me that now that he knows she's alive, she doesn't want him out of her life. Even though her life was going to be cut short.

She tells me that her grandpa asked her to call him Papa. She says she agreed as long as the word Beatrice never crossed his lips again. They shook on it. Anybody that is anybody knows you don't go back on something you shook on.

On our fourth loop around the neighborhood, we see the front door to Bea's papa's house open. Her dad puts his hand out to shake her papa's hand, and her papa pulls him in for a hug instead. They both look like they're crying.

Beatrice

They're crying. I think that's a good sign. They're not yelling at each other, also a good sign. We walk over, and my papa says, "Bea, if it's alright with you, I'd love for you to come by again to play cards with me. I think I need a rematch. Your friend Chloe should come too."

With no hesitation, I say, "I'd really like that. Maybe next weekend?"

Papa responds, "Perfect, Bea. I'll see you and your friend next weekend."

I say, "You sure will. But be prepared to lose at cards. I play to win."

"That, my dear, you must have gotten from me," he says.

We all laugh. I run up and give my new papa a hug. He kisses my head and says he wants to make up for lost time. I tell him I want that, too.

We get in the car, wave at Papa, and head back toward home.

On the ride home, my dad tells us he met with Mike's wife to continue with his investigation on Mike's death. His wife was hysterical. I guess anyone would be. The wife told my dad that two people showed up at her door a few days ago looking for Mike. He was on a fishing trip and wasn't supposed to return home for a few days.

When he left to go fishing, that was the last time she had spoken to her husband.

I asked Dad if he thought Mike was going to Mr. McBean's fishing cabin, but my dad wasn't sure if Ed even had a cabin. My dad said he couldn't find any records of Mr. McBean owning a fishing cabin. I tell my dad about Lenny saying someone bought it and rebuilt a big cabin. My dad shook his head and said he did not know of a new cabin being built.

For some reason, I can't stop thinking about the fishing cabin. I think we are missing something by not checking it out. What if Mr. McBean is there? Maybe he went to check it out, intending to come right back, but ended up sick or hurt. Or maybe he went there to hide out.

I tell my dad what I think, but he seems in a rush to get back to work. My dad drops us off at home and heads back to the station.

Chloe

I'm so happy that Bea is home. We decide to spend the day at the beach. On the way to the beach, we stop and grab an ice cream at Sunnys. Vic is at the diner, of course. I think she must sleep there.

"Hey, girls. How are we doing today?" Vic asks.

We answer at the same time that we are doing good. We start to giggle.

While we're waiting for our ice cream, we ask Vic what she thinks of Mike being murdered. We also ask if she has heard anything else about Mr. McBean. She seems annoyed that we are asking. Probably sick of hearing about it.

She tells us she doesn't know anything else than what she saw on TV. We ask her if Mr. McBean has a fishing cabin, and she seems to change the subject. Kind of odd. She tells us she's busy and has to get to the dishes.

We say we understand, although we don't, and walk out. We head toward the beach with our ice cream.

We end up sitting at the beach and spend the rest of the day talking and laughing. After some time, I ask Bea directly what the deal with my brother Owen is. Finally, Bea confirms what I thought was going on.

She tells me how much she likes him, how they held hands, and how he kissed her forehead.

While she was telling me, I couldn't help but see how her entire face lit up. She's so happy. I told her I was happy for her and Owen and hope things work out. I really hope they do. If nothing else, a relationship with Owen will keep her mind off everything else.

She asks me not to let on to Owen that I know anything. I pinky promised I wouldn't let on what I know. We spent the afternoon talking about how great it would be if Bea lives a long time and married Owen. That way, we will be more than best friends. We'd be family.

Beatrice

I'm so relieved that Chloe knows everything about Owen and me. I hated keeping things from my best friend. I was worried for nothing. She seemed so happy about me being with her brother. Even if it is only until I die. I can't wait to see Owen later on tonight.

We spent all day at the beach, decided to pack it up and go back to my house. We both need a shower and to get out of the sun. I know no one will be home since my dad is at the station and my mom had several house showings today. We figured we would go home, walk Peanut, take showers, and watch some TV.

We notice that something doesn't seem right when we walk up to the door. No cars are in the driveway, but the door is wide open.

I say, "Chloe, look at the door. Why would it be open? That's weird. My mom must not have realized she didn't close it all the way."

"Probably," says Chloe.

We go into the house, but something doesn't feel right. We don't hear Peanut. Usually, Peanut hears us and comes bounding over to see us. That's strange.

Chloe says, "Bea, did your dad take Peanut with him today?"

I give her a look of uncertainty. I hesitantly say, "He must have. There's no way Peanut wouldn't be climbing all over us if he were here."

We walk toward the kitchen to grab a drink before we take our showers. Chloe is chanting, 'Owen and Bea sitting in a tree, k-i-s-s-i-n-g.' We are both laughing, and I am telling her to stop. She keeps singing it over and over, 'Owen and Bea sitting in a tree, k-i-s-s-i-n-g.'

As soon as we get into the kitchen, Chloe screams.

Chloe

I scream, "Bea look."

Then Bea screams.

It's Peanut. He is lying on the floor in front of the stove, and he looks dead. He isn't moving. We run over and see if he's breathing. Bea says she thinks she can hear him breathing, but its super shallow. We don't know what to do. We're both crying, and Peanut isn't responding.

Bea runs to the phone to call her dad. Thankfully, I see Bea's mom pulling up in the driveway. She opens the door, running right in as soon as she hears how hysterical we are. She runs into the kitchen, panicked, asking what's wrong. Then she sees Peanut.

"Oh, my God. What happened to him?" she asks.

We tell her we have no idea. This is how we found him. One thing about Bea's mom is that she usually is pretty calm in scary situations. She tells us to go get a blanket from the closet. We grab a blanket and roll Peanut onto it. We need all of us to pick him up because he is dead weight.

We carry Peanut to her SUV and place him in the trunk. We all climb in and she races to the emergency vet office. She runs inside and comes out with the vet and the vet tech. They carry Peanut inside and tell us to have a seat and that they'll be out shortly.

We sit in the waiting area, and Bea and I are uncontrollably crying. Bea's mom keeps telling us to relax, wait, and see what the vet tells us. She keeps telling us that Peanut was breathing, so that was a good sign, and if anything can be done, they're in the right place.

It doesn't seem to help us relax. Peanut is such a good dog, and I can't imagine losing him.

Beatrice

How can this be happening? Peanut is the greatest dog. What could have happened? Maybe he had a heart attack. Do dogs even have those? Maybe he ate some chocolate? I know dogs aren't supposed to have chocolate. I don't even think we have any in the house. If we did, my dad surely would've eaten it by now.

This makes no sense. The woman behind the desk lets me use the phone, and I call my dad. I tell him what's going on, and he tells me he'll be right over. I'll feel so much better when he gets here.

After only ten minutes or so, my dad rushes in. We all update him on what happened. At least, how we got here because no one knows what happened yet to Peanut.

It takes the vet over an hour to come out from the back room. We all rush over as soon as we see him.

"Is he alright?" I say a smidge too loudly.

The vet responds, "For now. He still isn't out of the woods yet. He's a very sick dog, and you should all be prepared for the worst. He's comfortable right now and needs to stay here with us for the time being."

My dad asks, "Do you know what happened?"

The vet continues, "We aren't exactly sure what has happened yet. His blood pressure and heart rate were extremely low. We put him on IV fluids to bring his numbers up. His heart stopped a few times, and we were able to get it going again. There's no saying that it won't stop again. I took some blood samples and sent them to the local lab. Some symptoms Peanut is having could be from some type of neurological disorder or him eating something he shouldn't have. I administered activated charcoal to force him to empty his stomach."

"What could he have gotten into?" Chloe asks.

"Good question. Once we get the blood work back, we'll know more. I don't want to speculate without being sure. As soon as I get the results back, I'll give you a call. Chief? Is it okay for me to call the station with the update?"

"Actually, call the house number. I'm going to go home and wait for the call. Please keep me posted."

"Will do. For now, you guys should head home. As soon as I confirm what I believe has happened, I'll be in touch. I'm sorry, but I can't make any promises about his outcome."

We all tell him thank you and head out. We drive with my dad and my mom follows with her car. We head home and do nothing but wait. We all are quiet while we sit and wish the phone would ring with good news. I can't stop crying. Poor Peanut.

While we're waiting, my mom says, "Well, what are you going to do? If he doesn't make it, at least my house won't smell like a dog anymore."

I can feel my face get red. I am going to explode.

I scream, "I hate you." I run to my bedroom, Chloe at my heels.

I can hear my mom and dad fighting from my room. I can't believe how selfish she is. I sit there crying, and Chloe comes over, sits next to me, and puts her arm around me. She keeps telling me it'll be okay. This time when she whispers marshmallow, it doesn't seem to make me feel better.

I don't believe her.

Chloe

What a jerk Bea's mom is. She only thinks about herself. She's the polar opposite of her dad. He's the nicest person ever. I have no idea how he can stand her. She probably will be happy when Bea dies. She'll probably say something like, 'Well, at least we can save money on food and clothes.'

I actually thought she was going to say something comforting based on how she was at the vet's office.

Her mom and dad are downstairs. All you can hear is them screaming at each other. I'm not sure who, but one of them slams the door and leaves. I hope it's her. Maybe she'll never come back.

We stay in her bedroom until we jump up when we hear the phone ring. We run into the kitchen, and her dad is on the phone. He hangs up and says it was the wrong number. We head back to her bedroom, not even asking where her mom is.

About an hour later, the phone rings again. We both head to the kitchen, but not quite as fast as last time.

We hear her dad say a lot of, okay, I understand, keep me posted, makes sense, and I'll look into it.

Finally, he says thank you and hangs up.

"So, that was the vet. Peanut is responding well to treatment. He's not out of the woods yet, but showing some improvement. The blood work came back and showed that he had a poison in his system. It was antifreeze."

"What? How would he have gotten into that? He was in the house, and we don't have any of that around, right?" Bea asks.

"You're absolutely right, we don't have any antifreeze around. I can't understand how he could have gotten some."

"Wait. The door was open when we came home," I say.

"What? Today? When you found him unresponsive, the door was open?"

"Yes, I totally forgot with everything that was going on," Bea says.

"Maybe your mom forgot to close it. It makes no sense for someone to come in and give the dog a poison. There must be another explanation. Let's get something to eat and feel optimistic about Peanut's recovery. The vet is optimistic about how he's responding. Peanut must have found something in the yard or when we took him for a walk."

"You're probably right. I'm glad he seems better. I just want him home."

No one mentions Bea's mom not being home.

Beatrice

I don't even care if my mom comes home or not. I know that is mean to say, but she is so all about her. Right now, I don't need that in my life. I love my mom, but I hate how she acts sometimes. Maybe her not being home for a while is a good thing.

I ask my dad when she'll be coming home, and he says he doesn't know. He explains that they feel they need some time apart. She went to stay with her sister for a few days. He asks me what I think of it, and I tell him I think it is a good idea. He tells me he's not sure what will happen between the two of them. I let him know that no matter what, we'll be okay. He hugs me and tells me he loves me.

We order pizza for dinner, and my dad heads to the couch to watch a baseball game. Chloe and I go to my bedroom to get ready for bed. Then I remembered we never emptied our bag from the beach. We can't leave it because it has the food we didn't eat in it. I tell Chloe she can go get ready for bed. I'll empty the bag and be there in a few. She heads to my bedroom, and I head for the kitchen. It's quiet in here with Peanut not being here, that makes me sad.

I open up our lunch bag and see something strange. Under our not-eaten sandwiches is a card. At first, I'm hoping Owen left it. Then think I don't think he'd do that. Especially since he doesn't know Chloe knows what happened between us. Then I figure it is a cute card from Chloe. She has done super sweet things like that before. Besties for the resties. That must be it. I take the card and open the envelope.

Then I scream.

Chloe

I hear Bea screaming and run to see what's wrong. When I get to the kitchen door, Bea's dad is just getting there.

"What happened? Are you okay?" her dad asks.

"No. No, I'm not okay. Look."

In Bea's hand is a card. Her dad takes it and reads it. He says, "Are you kidding me?"

He reads it aloud.

"I TOLD YOU ONCE, LEAVE ED BE. THIS IS YOUR LAST WARNING. NEXT TIME I'LL FEED YOU THE POISON INSTEAD OF THE DOG!"

I can't stop shaking. Someone poisoned the dog on purpose. Who would do that? Clearly, the same person who told us to stop looking for Mr. McBean. This is insane. I can't believe someone would hurt Peanut. And threaten to hurt me and Bea. Obviously, we must be getting closer to finding Mr. McBean.

We sit at the table and Bea's dad tries to calm us down. He calls the station and has one of his deputies come over. He wants the card checked for fingerprints, and he wants the door also checked since it was left open. Most likely from someone coming in uninvited. My dad fills out a breaking and entering report. He sends us to my house for the night. He thinks we'll be safer over there.

We grab our stuff and run over to my house for the night. Bea's dad watches us the whole way over.

Beatrice

How is this possible? How could someone poison a dog? Someone broke into our house, fed Peanut poison, and left him to die. Why would someone think that was okay?

Clearly, we are getting closer to finding Mr. McBean. I have enough to worry about with dying from cancer than worrying over dying from someone else. This is so messed up.

Me and Chloe head to her room and talk about what's going on. Neither one of us saw anyone near our lunch bag. Who could have put the note inside it? We didn't leave the bag unattended at all, did we? We can't be sure.

Chloe's mom comes to her room to see if we are okay and asks what happened. We tell her what happened, and that we were scared. She goes to call my dad. When she comes up a little while later, she brings up some sleeping pills. She says she talked to my dad, and he said it was okay to take them. She thinks it'll help us both sleep. We take her advice, take the pills, and quickly fall asleep.

I dream I'm in a cabin on the water. Someone is yelling for me, but I can't make out who it is. Is it Chloe? My dad? I can't tell. Someone is holding me hostage. They're telling me I'm going to die. They tell me to drink the poison. I don't want to. I want to be left alone. I beg. I plead. I scream myself awake.

I am shaking. Chloe sits up next to me and hugs me. She tells me it will be okay and she will never leave me. Her mom comes into the room after hearing me scream. She tells us to come to her room, and we all climb into her king-sized bed and fall asleep.

Chloe

We spend the next week staying at my house. We check in with her dad a few times a day and he comes over to my house to see Bea. We don't leave the house. We watch TV, listen to music, do puzzles, eat, and sleep. Both of us are afraid to go out.

Peanut is still at the vet, hopefully he'll be able to come home in a few days.

Bea's mom is still staying with her sister. She hasn't called once to ask how Bea or Peanut are doing. That's kind of mean. I know it bothers Bea, but she doesn't like to talk about it. Her dad told her they were going to stay apart for the time being. He said they had a lot to work out before they could get back together. He made it clear that he wasn't exactly sure they would get back together. Bea didn't seem too surprised or upset about it.

Owen and Bea are getting closer and closer. Owen sat down with me and asked if it was okay for them to date each other. I had time to get used to the idea and told him I was so happy for them. I was glad they were together. I probably shouldn't have said it because now all they do is annoy me by being so smitten with each other. It makes me want to puke.

Bea hasn't been feeling too good lately. She seems to get tired easily and seems to always be in some pain. Her doctor gave her some different medications to try, but they made her super sleepy. Maybe being too sleepy is better than being in pain.

No one has heard anything about Mr. McBean. Still radio silence. Bea's dad said they are still looking for him and investigating his disappearance. No new leads in a while, but that's pretty expected in these types of cases.

Bea is getting closer to her new grandfather. They talk on the phone a lot. He wants to talk about the injections with her tomorrow. He's going to come to her house to meet with her and see what she thinks. He hasn't said he could help pay, so it's more whether or not she wants to try them.

Beatrice

It has been a lazy week. We haven't even left Chloe's house. It's refreshing to just do nothing. No looking for Mr. McBean, no rushing around town, and no Tommy issues. Just chilling with my best friend. We play cards, do puzzles, and stay in our jammies all day. Perfect.

My mom still isn't back home. I kind of doubt she'll ever come home. She hasn't once asked how I'm feeling since she left. Typical.

Peanut is on the mend. That makes me happy. The vet said we could pick him up soon.

I have no idea where Mr. McBean is. It's as if he vanished. My dad said they're getting closer to apprehending the prisoners. He also said the two sketchy people were still around, but the Harvard guy switched his sweatshirt to a Yale one. Still a far fetch based on his lack of intellect.

Owen is great. We talked to Chloe, and she was all in with me and Owen being together. He's so sweet. We have only kissed a few times since it seems like Chloe is always around. We're talking about going out on an official date soon. Just the two of us. I can't wait.

I just wish I felt better. Every day, I seem to have more pain and discomfort. I feel like all I do is sleep. I guess that's my body getting ready for endless sleep when I die. My papa is coming to see me tomorrow to talk about the injections. As of right now, I'm not interested. Now I just have to convince everyone else that it's a good plan.

For now, Chloe and I head to bed.

Chloe

I woke up and looked over. Bea is still sleeping next to me. She is so perfect. I don't know how I am going to survive when she's gone. I may not.

Besties for the resties. I just wish the resties would last longer.

Beatrice

I woke up, and Chloe was staring at me. I tell her to stop being so creepy. We both start laughing. We get up and head to the kitchen for breakfast. Her mom is making waffles for us with chocolate chips. My favorite. Owen already left for work. We're supposed to go to a movie tonight, just the two of us.

After breakfast, we head to take showers, and get dressed for the day. My papa is going to be here soon. My dad said after I talked to my papa to walk home with him since he wants to talk to both of us too.

We only have to wait a few minutes, and the doorbell rings. It's my papa.

I open the door. "Papa. I missed you. Come on in. This is Chloe's house. You remember Chloe, right?"

"Of course, I remember Chloe. I am old, but not that old. Is there a place we can sit and talk?"

"Sure. Let's go out back on the deck. Is it okay if Chloe comes too?"

"Of course she can come. Any friend of yours is a friend of mine."

We head out to the back deck. We make small talk as we wait for the coffee to brew for my papa. Chloe and I run in to grab a juice from the fridge. Chloe's mom left us some banana bread. We cut some, put it on a plate, and head outside.

My papa starts, "Bea, I think we need to talk about the cancer injections. I think you need to decide whether you want to try them. No one can make that decision but you."

Chloe says she is going inside and that this is a conversation we need to have together.

"I don't know what I should do. I know I don't want to extend my life if all I have is pain, but I also don't want to miss the opportunity if I can be cured. A twenty percent chance of being cured isn't very good. What would you do?"

"I think only you can make that decision. I can tell you a story that may make it clearer of a decision for you. Would you like to hear it?"

"I very much would like to hear it. Anything to help me make up my mind."

"A long time ago, there was this young man who was down on his luck and felt he had nowhere to go. He had no friends, no family and felt like life wasn't worth living. He decided the best thing to do was to end his life. He didn't think anyone would even notice if he was gone. He decided to go to the ocean and swim out as far as he could and let the waves take him. He was hopeless and felt that he had no purpose.

"One day, he walked to the beach and watched the waves to get ready to head in. As he was getting ready to make his way into the ocean, a girl walked onto the

beach. She was absolutely the most beautiful girl he had ever seen. She had the blondest hair, beautiful tan skin, and she was gorgeous. She looked over at him and smiled. She spread out her towel and sat down to enjoy the day.

"He couldn't help but stare at her. She was breathtaking. He knew, just by looking at her, that she was way out of his league and would want nothing to do with a lowlife like him. He brushed off her smile as a pity smile. He knew she would laugh at him if he went over to her.

"He started toward the ocean, ready to dive in. He stopped and said to himself, what do I have to lose? I could at least say hello. What's the worst thing that could happen? She may tell him to take off and want nothing to do with him. She may want to meet this lowly man. Only one way to find out. He took a chance and walked over to the most beautiful girl in the world. He walked over hesitantly.

"When he reached her, he dropped his head and said, 'I know I would never be good enough for you. But I want you to know you are the most beautiful girl in the world.'

"The woman asked him to pick his head up and look into her eyes. He did as he was asked. She smiled at him and said, 'You are worth more than you can ever know. I fear I am not worthy of you.'

"He looked into her eyes and said, 'That is impossible. You are more than enough.'

"She asked him to sit down next to him. She asked him not to go into the water. She said she had a feeling he was going to end his life. She said it wasn't his time. She said her name was Beatrice.

"That, my dear girl, was your grandmother. If not for taking a chance, we would never have met and fell in love. That day changed my life. Bea, it only takes one small chance to change the future. Don't throw that away because of fear.

"Embrace the challenge. Take a chance. Do everything it takes to test fate. If it doesn't work, then so be it. But don't sit back and think of what could have been. I was nothing without your grandmother. She made me know what life could be. All because I took a chance."

I couldn't help but cry. My papa shared a story so raw and full of emotion with me. If he could go against the odds and take a chance, then so could I.

I told him that based on his story and going against the odds, I would like to try the injections. He said he was proud of me and that my grandmother would have been proud of me, too. He told me he had the money and would pay whatever was needed for me to try the medications.

I am so thankful for my papa being part of my life. I think he can teach me how to make him proud.

Chloe

I knew the right thing to do was give Bea and her papa some space. I didn't want to, but I knew I should. I hope that he'll talk her into trying the injections. It might be her only chance to fight to live. All I want is for her to beat cancer and live a long, healthy life, being my best friend. Maybe even her being my sister-in-law. I can't imagine anything better.

I know it's unlikely that the injections will cure her cancer, I'm not stupid, after all. Why can't she be like the twenty percent of the people the injections helped? She doesn't have to be like the other eighty percent of the people.

If there were a God up there, you would think he would see how great she is and how much she would be missed if she were gone. She has a lot of life to live. I don't know if I can do it without her.

She comes running inside and tells me she has made a decision. She wants to try the injections. I'm so happy. I run over, hug her, and start crying my eyes out. I run out and hug her papa, too. I tell him thank you for whatever he said to Bea to change her mind. All he said was that her grandmother guided her. Whoever it was, I was so relieved.

Beatrice

I had no idea that Chloe would respond to the news of me trying the injections like that. She's jumping, crying, and yelling 'hooray' all at once. I don't think I've ever seen her so happy. Even when Ben from school told her she looked cute. I thought she was off the wall then. That was nothing compared to this.

We take my papa next door, into my house. My dad is there waiting for us. We told him what I decided. He seems so relieved. He tells me he thinks I should call my mom and let her know. I called my mom, and she said that she was happy that I decided to take a chance. She tells me she misses me. I actually believe her when she says it.

She tells me she and my dad are going to go to therapy and work on their marriage. I tell her that makes me happy. I tell her I do miss her being home, and for some reason, I actually mean it.

My dad takes the phone and calls Dr. Skinner. I hear him tell her my decision. He also says that my papa will pay for the treatments. She says she's happy that I've made the right decision. They agree for me to go in next week for my first injection.

I'm scared to start the injections, but I know they are worth the chance to get better and beat this horrible disease.

Chloe

I know this week has been super stressful for Bea. Waiting for the injections to start has been the worst. We spend most days hanging in my house or her house, just waiting.

Peanut came home a few days ago and is doing great. We are terrified of leaving him alone, since we have no idea who would poison a dog. Obviously, a very cold individual. We keep Peanut with us and don't let him out of our sight.

Bea's parents have started therapy and seem to be doing well. Her mom moved back home, and she seems less self-absorbed. I think the separation was a great wake-up call for her. Bea's mom and her grandpa have been getting together, too. They're trying to move forward in their relationship. So far, so good.

Bea has been feeling worse and worse each day. She seems to nap a lot during the day. She seems like she's in constant pain. I'm praying that the injections help her feel better. She never went out on a date with Owen. She hasn't felt well enough to go. I heard her tell him that once she feels better, they can go. I just hope that happens soon.

No news on Mr. McBean yet. The two prisoners were apprehended and were back in custody. They say they had nothing to do with Mike being killed. But I don't know if anyone believes them. I mean, they are in prison, so not too sure if they are super trustworthy. The investigation is still ongoing. The two creepy guys haven't been around for a few days, either. I'm glad they are gone, but I wonder what they're up to. Whatever it is, it can't be good.

Beatrice

Today is the day. The day of my first injection. I'm so nervous. Believe it or not, my mom is taking me to the appointment. She never would've taken me if not for the counseling.

My dad is working today, he has a few leads on Mr. McBean to look into. Chloe is going to stay home so that she can stay with Peanut. Almost losing him has made us know we never want to feel that way again.

My mom comes downstairs to the kitchen and asks if I'm ready to go.

I respond, "As ready as I will ever be."

My mom sits down next to me and hugs me.

She says, "Bea, before we go, I want you to know that I'm so proud of you. I know this has been very difficult for you. No matter what happens, we'll get through it together. I love you so much and am sorry for how selfish I've been. Working so much, running, and appointments were my way of distancing myself from the unknown. Can you ever forgive me?"

"Mom, there's nothing to forgive. I'm glad you are going with me today. I love you, too. Let's go get this done."

It takes us about an hour to get to the hospital. After waiting a short time in the waiting room, we're led into Dr. Skinner's office.

"Hi, Beatrice, Mrs. Chase. I'm so glad you are giving the injections a chance. The data from the trial shows significant results. I also have good news, I just heard from the hospital's philanthropy department, and they're using donations they've received to pay for your injections for the first three months. I approached them with your prognosis and information, and they're happy to help."

"Holy cow! I can't believe it. Thank you so much," I emphatically respond.

It's unbelievable that they're going to pay for the injections. Why would they pick me? It's amazing. I can't help it and I start to cry.

"Okay, Beatrice, let me show you how to give yourself the injections. I want to review some of the risks we've talked about before. There have been some people with fertility issues, and liver and kidney issues. We'll be doing weekly blood work to stay on top of your labs. I set this up to be done at your local hospital, so you don't have to trek up here once a week. Does that sound okay?"

I wipe the tears from my eyes and say, "It does. I'm ready."

Dr. Skinner brings in the vials of medication and syringes. She shows me how to draw up the medication into the syringe, prep the area on my thigh, and inject *the medication. Super easy and it doesn't even really hurt too much.*

I say, "Well, that was a quick ten thousand dollars."

We all laugh at that, and Dr. Skinner walks us out. She tells me I need to do the injections once a week and schedules me for blood work in one week. She makes a follow-up appointment with me in two months. She says if I'm feeling worse or had any reactions to the injection to call her office immediately. She also says if she sees anything concerning in the blood work, she will be in touch.

We walk out, and both of us are feeling optimistic. Only time will tell. My mom takes me out to lunch in the city. I'm feeling good, hopeful.

Chloe

Finally, Bea is home. It was the longest day ever. No one likes waiting, me especially. I so hope the injection went well. I know it was a huge decision for Bea to make. I'm just so happy she chose to fight. This has to work.

As soon as her mom puts the car in park, I run over to see Bea. She opens the door and I start to cry. I can't help it. I'm so happy she's home.

"If you're going to cry every time you see me, I'm going to stop coming home. Dial down the crazy, will ya?"

We both start laughing. She always has a way to make me laugh. She tells her mom we're going to go grab chocolate shakes from Sunnys. She actually says she wants one too.

Bea asks if she'll sit with Peanut while we go grab the drinks and come back with them. She says that's great. She'll be waiting on the back deck with the dog. She says she has a call to make, so that will work out perfectly.

Bea and I walk to the diner.

We get to the diner and see Kyle and Rachel sitting at the counter. We walk over and sit down next to them.

"Hi, Rachel. Hi Kyle. How are you guys?" Bea asks.

Rachel doesn't even acknowledge our existence, but Kyle says all is good. He tells us they're trying to enjoy the nice weather and probably going to head to the beach. Bea asks Rachel if she has heard anything about her dad. She looks over at Bea and says, "Nope, and I don't care."

Bea says, "You know, take it from me. Life is too short. I'm dying of cancer and have little hope for a future. Your time on this planet is never guaranteed, and not being there for your dad over a guy is stupid. He's your dad, after all. I can't imagine not having a relationship with my dad. No guy is worth that. Sorry, Kyle, no offense."

Kyle says, "None taken. I know her dad and I don't see eye to eye, but I think Rachel should be closer to her dad, too."

Rachel responds, "I get what you're saying. I can't do anything with him missing or dead, can I? I lost my chance to work things out, and I have to live with that. I don't need a lecture today."

She gets up and walks out. Kyle tells us he has to go be with her. He asks if we hear anything about her dad to let them know. He thinks Rachel is just trying to protect herself if he's never found. He gets up to follow Rachel.

Bea looks at me and says, "Is it possible Kyle isn't the tool we thought he was?"

We both look at each other and at the same time say, "No, that can't be it."

We are laughing like crazy people when Vic spies us and comes over.

"Hey there, girls, haven't seen you two in a while? Not feeling good, Bea?"

Bea responds, "Yeah, I haven't been feeling too good. Tired. How's everything with you?"

"Oh yeah, ya know, living the dream. What can I grab you two?"

We order three chocolate shakes and start to talk about Mr. McBean. It's been a while since Bea has felt up to talking about him. We talk about how the prisoners have been captured, how the two weird guys haven't been around, and how Lenny hasn't been around either.

Vic comes over with our shakes, and we ask her if she has seen Lenny or the two sketchy guys around. She tells us she hasn't seen Lenny and figures he's busy at the shop. She says the two guys haven't been around either. She asks why we are so interested in finding Mr. McBean anyway. She says some things are better left alone.

We have no response to that and head for the door. She yells to us, "Some things are better left dead and buried."

Beatrice

We walk out and walk down the street. Both of us are dumbstruck.

I say, "Did she really just say that? Did she just say some things are better left dead and buried? What the heck? Who said he was dead? Something definitely isn't right."

Chloe responds, "I totally agree. Something isn't adding up. Maybe she's just venting because she's sick of hearing about him being missing. I actually think he is probably dead. Whoever killed Mike probably also killed Mr. McBean. Someone may have wanted them to stay quiet."

"Chloe, you're probably right. I think I know what we need to do, but I'm not sure you are going to like it."

"Oh boy, now I'm scared."

We get to my driveway and I tell Chloe that we'll talk about it later. I tell her I don't want my mom to know, or my dad either, for that matter.

Chloe says, "Marshmallow." I giggle.

Chloe

Yup, I'm terrified.

We head to the back deck with our shakes and Bea's mom is just getting off the phone. We sit down, and each takes a shake. It's a beautiful day that I wish would never end. Especially now that I'm afraid of what Bea's plan is.

Bea's mom starts talking about the upcoming school year. School starts in a few weeks, and I'm so not looking forward to it. Mostly because Bea won't be there. Her doctor told her she's not cleared to go back to school yet. So I'll be on my own.

I dread seeing Tommy and Angela. I dread doing schoolwork on my own. I dread eating lunch by myself. But, mostly, I dread not hanging with Bea. This has been the best summer, the 'Summer of C,' well, except for looking for a dead guy.

Beatrice

Finally, my mom tells us she has to go show a few houses and won't be back until suppertime. She gets up, grabs her purse, and heads out.

"I thought she'd never leave," I say

"Okay, Bea, what's the plan? I'm afraid I may not want to know. Is it bad?"

"Nope, just scary," I say.

"Great. Just what I was hoping for, not," Chloe says.

"So, I think we need to bring our search for Mr. McBean up a notch. Here's what I think, if Mike was part of the fraud and was killed, then maybe the same thing happened to Mr. McBean. I think maybe if Mike and Mr. McBean came to the same fate, that maybe they were both dumped at the same place.

"It makes sense for us to go to Hemlock Lake, look around, and see if we can find Mr. McBean's body. We can spend the afternoon hiking around the lake and see if we can find anything. My gut is telling me he's probably there, probably dead. I think it would be good if we could find his body and let him be properly laid to rest. The scary part is I really am not ready to see a dead body. That and walking in the woods where there are bugs and stuff. What do you think?"

Chloe takes a few minutes to think about it before she responds. She finally says, "Bea, I may be sorry, but I think you're right. We need to go look. Now the question is, how do we get there?"

"Good question, Chloe. Good question."

We sit on the deck with our shakes and try to figure out how to get out to the lake. It's not crazy far, but certainly too far for us to ride our bikes. We decided we needed to bring Peanut with us, too. We're both afraid to leave him alone.

We sit for a bit and try to see who would take us out to the lake and whom we trust.

I start with, "How about Rachel? Can we trust her to take us? She says she doesn't want to see her dad again, but if pressed, she probably would feel like she has to take us."

Chloe says, "Maybe, not sure about her, though. She is a little unpredictable. Who else?"

"How about Lenny? He was friends with Mr. McBean, so you'd think he would want to go. That is, if he isn't too busy at the shop."

"That could work. Can you call the shop and see if he's around?" Chloe suggests.

"Be right back. Let me see if he's there."

Chloe

While I'm waiting for Bea, I keep thinking, who else can help? It's pretty limited who we can ask. She doesn't want her mom and dad to find out, so we can't ask a deputy for a ride. The bus doesn't go that far, so Stu is out. Vic is working, so I don't think she could take us.

My brother would be perfect, but he's most likely working. He's trying to save money for college. Lenny might be our only hope. Actually, I would love to take Tommy out there and leave him to fend for himself. That makes me smile, thinking about how hurt he could get.

Bea comes back and asks what I'm smiling about. I say nothing. This image I'll keep to myself for now.

"Okay then, whatever, don't tell me. I called the shop, and Lenny didn't answer. He probably is under a car doing a repair. I did leave a message and tell him what we were up to. I asked him if he gets the message and wants to meet us to help look that it would be great."

"Are you sure you trust him? Remember, he lied about talking to Mike and about the lighter being his?"

"True, but I think he's a nice guy who's just confused about stuff. He's harmless, and another set of eyes looking can only help. Hemlock Lake is pretty big."

"You're right, Bea. Anyone else we can call? I thought about my brother, but I'm sure he's working. He has picked up so many hours lately."

"Oh my God, Chloe, you're a genius. I didn't even think of him. He has been working a lot, which is one reason we still haven't gone out on a date. But, lucky for us, his car is in your driveway."

"Are you kidding? He's home? Let's go see if he'll take us."

Beatrice

We grab Peanut, his leash, and run over to Chloe's house. Her mom is in the kitchen baking cookies. She tells us they'll be ready in a few minutes. We tell her we want to talk to Owen. She says he's in his room.

We blast to his room and knock on his bedroom door.

"Come in," he yells.

We open the door, and he's sitting on his bed watching TV. God, he's so cute. I could look at him all day.

He immediately starts blushing and says, "Hi, Bea. Hey, Chloe. What's up?"

Chloe asks him why he isn't working today. He tells us the manager is making him take the day off. He says the manager thinks he's been working too hard.

"That makes sense," Chloe says.

We sit on the side of his bed and tell him what we're thinking. We tell him we think Mr. McBean probably is already dead, but we want to go search for him. He offers to drive us and help us look.

I'm so happy to be spending time with him. Hiking in the woods is going to be fun, even if we're looking for a dead body.

We tell Chloe's mom that we are going to the park. We don't want her to worry. We grab some drinks in a cooler, Peanut, and head for the door. Chloe's mom stops us and gives us cookies to take. This is going to be a great day. Well, not for Mr. McBean, but for us.

We load up in the car. Owen makes Chloe and Peanut sit in the back. He says he wants me to sit up front next to him. I can't stop smiling.

Chloe

Owen and Bea. I'm happy for her, but Owen, really? I guess I don't see it. Probably because I've seen him as only being a stupid brother, who I've seen pick his nose, not shower for days, and wet his bed. I don't see him as being a catch, but whatever. But, they do seem like a cute couple, if I take the gross brother images from my mind.

It takes us about twenty minutes to get to Point Street, which is at the end of Hemlock Lake. Hemlock Lake is a great spot to hike, kayak, canoe, and fish. There are some really nice houses around the lake and some really small cabins that have been there for years. There are tons of hiking paths that go around the lake. It certainly is too big to cover in one day.

As we go down the street, Bea yells, "STOP!"

Owen pulls off the side of the road and says, "What happened? What's the matter?"

Bea tells us when we were talking with Carl from the nursing home, he said something about Mr. McBean's cabin being at the orange marker on the tree. She points to the left side of the street, at the big oak tree, and sure enough, there's a big orange marker.

I say, "Wow, good catch, Bea. I think this is a great place to start then."

We park the car, grab Peanut and a few waters, and start our search.

Beatrice

Well, here we go. We walk along and follow the path toward the water. We're not exactly sure where they found Mike's body, but before long, we see yellow police tape that was left by a tree. We figure we must be in the right place.

Peanut is running around the woods, and Chloe is a few steps ahead of us. Owen reaches over and grabs my hand. We walk along, hand in hand, through the woods. This day can't get any better.

We spend a few hours walking around, but see nothing. The woods are pretty dense and hard to see too far ahead. We stopped a few times for a drink of water and a few cookies. Peanut seems to be loving life. Not quite as much as me, but still loving life.

After another hour, we decided we should probably head back toward the car since it was getting close to dinnertime. Owen asks if anyone has seen Peanut.

"He was just here. Where did he go off to?" I say.

We all start yelling for Peanut. He couldn't have gone too far. We keep walking toward the lake, continuing to yell for Peanut. Finally, we hear him bark. We all go running toward the noise. He barks a few more times as we make our way toward him. Something is bothering him for sure. Then we hear him yelp. Holy cow, that isn't good. We need to find Peanut. The whining gets louder. We start to run toward the noise.

About 100 feet further, we see Peanut. It was him whining. He is lying on his side, just lying there.

Chloe yells, as she is running over to him, "What happened? Peanut, are you okay?"

"Is he okay?" I say.

We all get to Peanut's side and sit around him. We're all looking him over, trying to see what's wrong. Owen lifts up Peanut's head, and there's blood on the ground.

"What happened? How did he get hurt? Do you think he fell and hit his head? That's a lot of blood," I say.

This cannot be happening. I start to shake. This cannot be real.

Owen says, "Chloe, run back to the car and grab a blanket and some towels. I have some in the trunk. We have to stop the bleeding and try to carry him out. We can use the blanket to lift him up."

Chloe says nothing. She just jumps up and runs back toward the car.

Owen takes off his shirt and puts it under Peanut's head. Peanut is still whimpering and panting. Poor baby. "Please don't die, Peanut, stay with us," I say.

Owen takes my hand and says it'll be all right. I so want to believe him, but I don't.

Chloe

I run as fast as I can. It's hard because of all the roots and sticks on the ground. Peanut must've fallen or tripped over something and hit his head. That was a lot of blood. We have to get the bleeding to stop and get Peanut to the vet.

I see the car up ahead. Thank god, I found it. Wait, there's a truck parked next to Owen's car. I wonder who else is here. Hopefully, they'll be able to help.

"Lenny? Is that you?" He doesn't need to answer because, by the time he hears me, I'm running up to him.

"Lenny. Thank god you're here. Peanut's hurt in the woods, and we're going to need help getting him to the car."

I grab the towels, water, and the blanket from Owen's trunk and get ready to run back. Lenny isn't saying anything. He's a bit of an oddball.

"Lenny, let's go. We need help."

As I turn and start toward the woods, Lenny says, "Hold on a second. I have to get something out of the truck."

"Okay, Lenny, but hurry. It's bad up there, we don't have time to waste."

Beatrice

Owen is holding his T-shirt to Peanut's head to put pressure on the wound. There's a lot of blood, and it's hard to see how bad the injury is. Peanut's breathing has slowed, and it's really shallow. I don't think he'll make it much longer. I wish Chloe would get back already. What the heck is the hold-up?

"Owen, do you think Peanut is going to be okay?"

"I don't know, Bea. I can't really see how bad it is, but it sure is bleeding a lot. Chloe should be here in a few minutes. Hey Bea, what's that over there? Am I seeing things, or is that a cabin?"

"Where? I don't see anything. Oh, wait, over there across the way. There is something there. It's hard to tell what it is. It could just be trees that fell over. I'm going to run over and see what it is, okay? If it's a cabin, maybe it's open, and I can grab something we can use to get Peanut to the car."

"Sounds good. Be careful." Owen says.

"I will. I'll be right back."

I lean over Peanut and give Owen a quick kiss. I don't know why I kiss him, maybe just to let him know how happy I am that he's with me.

"If you keep that up, I may not let you go."

I blush.

I ran off toward whatever it was in the woods we saw. I can't tell what it is until I get pretty close to it. It is a cabin. It's in rough shape. It doesn't look like anyone has been here in forever. I bet this is Mr. McBean's fishing cabin. Its right about where Carl told us it would be.

If it weren't for Peanut getting hurt, we'd never have found it. It's covered with brush and falling tree limbs. I walk around the cabin to get to the front door.

I try the door, but it's locked. It doesn't matter too much since one window is broken. Not even broken, just not there at all. It's kind of creepy, and I'm slightly afraid of looking inside. This would've been much better for Chloe to handle, she's the brave one.

I peek into the window hole and try to look inside. It takes my eyes a minute to adjust to the darkness inside. It's pretty bare inside. There's a very small sink and countertop. A gross, dirty couch and not much else. On the couch is an old, ratty-looking blanket. Yes. A blanket. I'll just go in quick, grab the blanket, and rush back to Owen. Sweet Owen.

I put my head through the window opening and reach around to unlock the door. It takes me a minute to unlock it. Once unlocked, I push open the door and hesitantly step inside. It looks like no one has been here for ages. There are cobwebs everywhere. It smells gross, like someone died in here.

I walk over as quickly as I can to the couch to grab the blanket when something rubs against my ankle. I scream. My heart is about to explode. I look down to see what it is, but don't see anything. Once I stop freaking out and my heart rate goes back to normal, I look again.

Then I see it, a kitten.

I reach down, pet the tiny kitten, and tell him it'll be okay. I pick him up. He's so sweet. I'm sure he's covered with fleas, but I don't even care. He needs me. Before I leave, I look around and make sure there aren't any more kittens around. I peek under the couch and don't see any others. The space isn't very big, and it looks like he is the only one.

I grab the kitten and the blanket, and start toward the door. The kitten jumps out of my arms and darts toward the back of the cabin. The kitten sits in front of a closed door. I didn't even notice the door. I pick up the kitten. I give the kitten a hug. He's the cutest thing ever.

I wonder if there are more kittens behind the door. God, I wish Chloe was here. I slowly open the door and peek inside. I drop the kitten and the blanket and scream as loud as I can.

My inside voice is saying marshmallow.

Chloe

"Come on, Lenny, let's go." I am getting antsy. What's taking him so long? Finally, he walks over and says, let's go. We walk along. I'm carrying the blanket, water, and the small towels. Lenny asks if I need help. I said no.

We walk along in silence. I get lost along the way and have to backtrack in order to find my way. I finally see Owen sitting with Peanut up ahead. We keep walking and come up to Owen. I don't see Bea.

"Owen. I'm back, and I found Lenny. He's going to help. Where did Bea take off to? We need to get Peanut out of here."

Right then, we hear the scream. That's Bea. I'd know her scream anywhere.

"Oh my God, Owen, that's Bea. Where is she? Something's wrong. We need to find her."

"Not so fast. I think we need to sit and wait here," Lenny says.

We look over at Lenny and for some reason, he's standing there with something in his hand.

It's a gun.

And it's pointed right at us.

Beatrice

I can't stop screaming. All I can see is a blanket covering something on the floor, and a human foot is sticking out. I knew something was dead in here. I can't catch my breath. I need Chloe.

Who's under the blanket? I am afraid to look. I need to calm down. What if the person isn't dead? I should lift the corner of the blanket and peek. Oh, God help me. I'm so scared. I tell myself, you can do this. It'll be okay. Try to be brave like Chloe, just lift the corner, and see who it is. See if they're dead.

I inch over cautiously. I slowly lean down and put my hand on the corner of the blanket. I have to tell myself that I can do this. The kitten comes over and nudges my hand. You're right, little kitten, we can do this.

I lift the corner of the blanket just enough so I can look under. It's definitely a person. He looks dead. It's Mr. McBean. I'm so sad. I knew he was probably dead, but I didn't think it would be like this. I was so hoping I would find him alive. This is horrible. Who could've done this to him?

Chloe

"Lenny. What the heck are you doing? What's going on? Put the gun away."

"Don't tell me what to do. I'm in charge now. You couldn't stop looking for Ed, could ya? No matter how many warnings you were given. Just couldn't leave things alone. Where's Bea? It would be good if you were all together for what's going to happen next."

"Lenny, are you serious? What are you doing? Just leave us alone. We won't say anything about Ed. Whatever you did, we'll pretend we didn't see anything. You don't want to hurt us. Especially Bea. She has always been nice to you."

"Keep quiet. Do you actually think I can trust you guys to keep quiet? You have disregarded all the warnings so far. You just couldn't leave Ed alone. He was not worth you looking for him. That's for sure."

"You were supposed to be his friend. Why would you hurt him?" I say.

"You think you know Ed? Well, you don't. So much for him being my friend. He steals money from the mill and flaunts it around me all the time. When I need a loan, he says no. What a great friend. I hope he rots in hell. The world is a better place without him in it."

"You killed him for money? Is money so important to you that you'd kill someone for it? I can't believe you would do that. I thought you were a hardworking guy, not a murderer."

"Well, I guess you don't know me so well. Leave the dog and let's go."

"Where're you taking us?" Owen asks.

"We're going to find your precious friend, Bea."

He points the gun at us and pushes us further into the woods.

Beatrice

The kitten runs under the blanket.

"Here kitty, here kitty. Come out of there," I call, trying to coax the kitten out.

The kitten peeks out from under the blanket, and I put my hand under to grab him. "Come on, little guy." My hand is under the kitten, and as I'm trying to get a grip on the kitten, something grabs my hand. I drop the kitten and fall backward. I look over and see Mr. McBean's dead hand move. I think I may vomit.

The hand moves ever so slightly.

Oh my God, he's alive. Mr. McBean is alive. I quickly pull off the blanket and see his eyes are open. He's crying. He looks horrible. I tell him I found him and I'm going to get help. His voice is super weak. He takes my hand and whispers, "Thank you, Bea."

I have never been so happy to see someone. He is alive. Now I just have to figure out how to get him out of here. I tell him I am going to get help. I tell him to wait right where he is. As soon as I say it, I realize he doesn't have very much choice. I tell him I'll be right back, and I run out to get Owen.

I bolt out of the door and see Owen and Chloe heading over to me. Thank God.

"Guys, I'm so happy you're here. I need help. Lenny? Is that you? I am so glad you got my message."

Then I see the gun, and it's pointed straight at the back of Chloe's head. I scream.

Owen and Chloe, what the hell is going on? I can't stop shaking my head in disbelief. This can't be right. Lenny, sweet Lenny, did this to Mr. McBean and killed Mike. Why would he do that? I don't understand.

I ask a lot of questions, and Lenny tells me everything. About how it was all about the twenty-five thousand dollars and how he hated how Ed flaunted his cash but wouldn't help him out. He said he did what he had to. It still makes no sense. By the way he's talking, I don't think he realizes that Mr. McBean is still alive.

I try to distract him from going any further toward the cabin, since I'm well aware of our fate if we make it in there.

"Did you know the prisoners would get blamed?" I ask.

"Of course I did. Why do you think I chose then to take care of him? Mike tried to get in the way, so he had to be taken out, too. Everyone thinks Ed was so smart by getting the free money and doing no time, but they didn't count on me being smarter. Let's go. Keep walking, or I'll have to shoot poor Chloe."

We walk in front of Lenny and make our way toward the cabin. I hope Mr. McBean stays quiet and pretends to be dead because, if not, he will be soon.

I can't believe Lenny is behind all of this. And over money. He is totally crazy. How are we going to get out of here? Please, God, please help us.

Chloe

This is crazy. If only I had hidden and not told him where we were, he probably wouldn't have found us. I'm so stupid. No one knows we're up here looking, so no one will come for us. What are we going to do?

Poor Bea. She doesn't need this right now. She just had her first injection to try to save herself from cancer, and this nut bag is going to kill her. Please, God, please help us.

We walk ahead of Lenny further into the woods. I'm not sure where he is taking us, but it can't be good.

It happens so fast that no one sees it coming.

Peanut bolts over and jumps on Lenny. Lenny falls to the ground. This is insane. Lenny's screaming, trying to push Peanut off of him. Peanut isn't letting go. This is awesome.

Owen says he's going for help. He runs off back the way we came. Bea and I watch Peanut attacking Lenny. Lenny is yelling for the dog to get off of him. Peanut is not letting go. Bea runs over and grabs the gun. She points it at Lenny. There's a loud bang, and the gun goes off.

Peanut lets go of Lenny and runs off, away from the noise. I look at Bea and say, "Did you get him? Is he dead?"

Beatrice

I look at Chloe, confused, and say, "That wasn't me. I didn't fire the gun."

"What are you talking about? You have the gun. What did you do?"

"But she didn't shoot, I did," a voice says.

We both turn around to see who said it. Standing there, holding a gun pointing up to the sky, is someone we never expected to see.

Vic.

Chloe says, "Thank God you're here. How did you know we were here? Thank you so much for coming. I don't know what we would've done if you didn't show up."

"Ummm Chloe." I say, "I don't think Vic is here to help us. I think she may be here to hurt us." She looks like she could kill us. Something isn't right.

"Well, look at you, Bea, being super smart. I knew you were smart every time you came into my diner. All you kept doing was asking questions about Ed. You couldn't just leave it alone. I gave you plenty of warnings. Even so, you had to keep it up. Chloe here looks very confused. It's okay, Chloe. Let me explain.

"I'm not here to help you, I'm here to make you stop looking for Ed. I left the note at the beach, and that didn't stop you. I even poisoned Ed's stupid dog, and that

didn't work. You guys are giving me no choice but to get rid of you both. Lenny, get the hell up. You're fine. It's only a dog bite."

Lenny struggles to get up and asks where the other kid is. Vic seems shocked someone else was with them.

She yells to Lenny, "There was someone else with them? Well, what are you doing just sitting there? Go grab the gun and go look for him. What are you waiting for? Go get him and kill him."

"Why are you doing this? I don't understand. You're working for Lenny. That makes no sense," Chloe says.

"Oh Chloe, you are just not too smart, aren't you? I'm not working for Lenny, dear. Lenny works for me. He's merely a means to an end. Ed thinks he can take the money and not give any to me. Well, he's mistaken. I earned that money right along with him and deserved it as much as he did."

"Wait, you were the fourth person in the fraud scheme?" I ask.

"See, Bea, you are the smart one. Of course, I was the fourth person involved. You think Mike could've pulled it off? No way. It was my idea all along. All until Ed got a conscience and wanted to rat everyone out. He only never mentioned me because I threatened to kill his mother. The woman is so confused, it would have been easy to kill her.

"She thought I was Rachel the last time I saw her. I could totally have gone into the nursing home, killed her, and everyone would have thought she died of old age. Ed begged me to leave her alone. He would still be with us until he started saying how much worse his mother was and that it'd be a blessing if she would die already. Kind of like you, Bea. Shouldn't you be dead already?"

"You're evil. So not only did you want the money, but you also thought Ed was going to go to the cops and tell them of your involvement?"

"Exactly Chloe. See, now you're listening and finally getting up to speed. Good job."

"How did you get Lenny to help you? He doesn't seem as mean and evil as you?" Chloe asks.

"Good question. Poor stupid Lenny. He was friends with Ed until I started telling him lies about Ed, feeding him all kinds of lies about Mike, too, so he would hate both of them. I had to sick the two thugs you saw around to put the pressure on him. I paid them to hang around, look guilty, and tell Lenny that Ed hired him to get intel to set up Lenny. Worked like a charm. Two crazy people telling someone they were working against him was all Lenny needed to firm up the deal. He's like a child, so easy to manipulate."

"Do you really think you'll get away with this?"

"I have so far, haven't I? Do you really think that you two are going to stop me?"

"Stranger things have happened," I say.

Chloe

This is so crazy. Vic is the mastermind, and Lenny is the sidekick. I would never have guessed in a thousand years that Vic and Lenny could do this. I hope Owen makes it to the car and goes to get help for us. He has to move fast.

If Lenny catches up to him, he was told to kill Owen. Based on everything that has gone down, I actually think he will kill him. Lenny is probably terrified of Vic, as well as he should be. He was just a pawn in Vic's plan.

Vic tells us to get moving. She's behind us now, walking deeper into the woods the same way Lenny was taking us. I have no idea where we're going. Bea grabs my hand, and we walk next to each other. It looks like Bea is up to something, but I have no idea what.

We continue on, and I see a small cabin up ahead. She must be taking us up there. It looks like an old abandoned cabin. I don't think anyone has been here in years.

We hear someone walking in the woods. We can't see who it is, but we can hear the twigs breaking as someone is stepping on them. Bea turns around, stops, and looks at Vic.

Bea says, "Vic, how come you killed Mike? What did he do?"

I think she's stalling and doesn't want to go into the cabin. She must have seen what's inside, and if she doesn't want to go back, it must be bad.

"He figured out what was going on, and he was going to go to the cops. I think Ed couldn't help himself and told Mike what was going on. You know, Bea, your sweet old man, too bad he isn't here to protect you. I'm going to enjoy killing you two, just like I did to Mike and Ed. After I'm done with you two, I think I'll kill the dog too. How does that sound?"

We all hear someone walking toward us, and Vic says,

"Oh good, Lenny's back. That means he got the other one already. Lucky me, I don't have to waste a bullet on another one."

I'm so scared. I'm so hoping Owen got away. Vic is right. If Lenny didn't get to Owen, he would've followed him in his car and not come back to us. Poor Owen. Please let him make it for help. He has been gone for what seems like a long time. If he made it to his car and got to a phone, I would think help should be close.

"Lenny, about time you came back. You take care of our little escape artist?"

"No. He'd already left when I got to my truck."

"And why didn't you follow him, you idiot? He could go to the cops."

"Someone slashed my tires. I think maybe it was him."

"Ya think? God, you're useless. I can't believe I thought you could handle one thing. What exactly have you done to help me out? I had to kill Mike, I had to kill Ed, I had to poison the dog, and now I'm going to have to kill these two. You're useless."

Vic turns back to Chloe and me and tells us to get ready for fun. We have no idea what she's talking about. We hold each other's hands tighter.

She turns around and shoots Lenny in the chest. He falls to the ground and is motionless.

We both scream.

With Vic being distracted, I grab Bea's hand, and we run. I've never run so fast in my life. I actually hate running. I always said you would only see me running if someone was chasing me. I guess this is what I meant.

We try to stay together and run as fast as we can away from the cabin. We stop behind a tree and listen to see if Vic is getting closer. She's slower than we are, but she's yelling.

"Girls, time to stop running. I'll find you and kill you both. There's nowhere to hide. You have no way of getting back to civilization. No car, no people around, only soon-to-be two dead bodies buried in the brush."

We take off running again. This time, we don't stop. I can see Lenny's truck up ahead. Maybe he has another gun inside or something we can use as a weapon. I think Bea is thinking the same thing. We can hear Vic getting closer.

We reach the car and grab a tire iron from the bed of the truck. We don't see a gun, but we find a hunting knife sitting on the passenger seat. We sit on the ground, on the side of the truck that's not visible from the woods, and wait for our attacker.

I turn to Bea and whisper, "Besties for the resties."

She grabs my hand and squeezes it.

Beatrice

We're both sitting next to each other at the side of the truck. We're shaking.

In a super quiet voice, I say, "Chloe, if we don't make it out of here, I want you to know how much I love you, and I'm so glad we're best friends."

Chloe says, "We are getting out of this. We have to."

I believe her.

All we can do is sit and wait. Since Vic keeps yelling for us, we have an idea of how close she is to reaching us. She's getting closer. I tell Chloe to get ready to fight. I have the knife, and Chloe has the tire iron.

I tell Chloe that when she sees Vic come around the truck, to stay low and hit her in her knees, that'll make her fall, and I'll use the knife to stop her. We give each other a hug and wait.

She's creeping up closer. We can see legs from under the truck getting closer. She's nearing the back bumper. We're ready. She steps around the truck, she's in view. Wait, that's not Vic. That's my dad.

"Dad! What are you doing here? It's Vic, watch out."

"It's okay, Bea. She's in custody. She won't be hurting anyone again."

"But, how? How did you find us? Where is she?"

"Everything is alright girls. Owen called the station from a house up the road and told me Lenny was

holding a gun on you two. We came around the backside of the lake and saw and heard everything she said. We also saw her shoot Lenny. He's en route to the hospital now. Are you two hurt?"

"No, but Dad, Mr. McBean."

"I know, Bea. I heard Vic confess to killing him, too."

"No, Dad. Mr. McBean, he's alive. He's in the cabin. I told him I was going to get help. He doesn't look so good, but he's alive."

My dad picks up his radio and tells his deputy to get over to the cabin immediately. He tells them to look for Mr. McBean. He then calls for an ambulance to meet him at the cabin. He asks if we're going to be all right. He says he needs to get to the cabin. We both get up and say, "Not without us."

We keep up with my dad as we race toward the cabin. We get there just as the deputy and ambulance arrive. We run in, and I show my dad where Mr. McBean is. We find him, and he's sitting up.

My dad shows the EMTs where he is. They get him on a gurney and are wheeling him out of the cabin. He grabs my hand and mumbles, "I knew if anyone was going to find me, it'd be you, Bea. Great detective work."

I give him a hug, and they take him for transport. After the ambulance leaves, my dad says he wants us to go to the hospital and be checked out. We both say we're fine and want to go home. First, we need to see if we can find Peanut. He's out there somewhere. My dad says he'll help us look.

As we're leaving the cabin, I hear a very soft meow. I look over, and the little kitten is sitting there next to my feet. I lean down to pick him up, and he runs to the room Mr. McBean was found in. I run in after him. Sitting on the floor is another kitten. They look exactly the same. They are black and white. I pick them both up.

"Is that what you were trying to show me before? Is this your little friend? Well, we can't leave a friend behind, can we? Let's go."

I hope Peanut is prepared to meet kittens. We shall see.

I hand a kitten to Chloe, and we walk out to look for Peanut.

The kittens both are nuzzling our necks as we walk along.

My dad says, "And who do we have here?"

"Looks like we both will have new additions to the family," I say.

We both giggle.

My dad says, "Looks that way. Now let's go find Peanut."

Chloe says, "Someone just has to convince my mom and dad that I need a new kitten."

I respond, "How can anyone say no to such a cute face?"

We walk through the woods and keep calling for
Peanut. A few minutes later, one of the deputies calls us
over. He found something. He found Peanut.

Chloe

He found Peanut. He's alive. His tail is wagging. He looks so happy to see us. His head is wet with blood, but it doesn't look like it's bleeding right now. He gets up and goes over to Bea to see what she's holding. Apparently, Peanut isn't a huge fan of the kitten. He seems a bit confused about what the furry thing is. We all head to Bea's dad's cruiser and drive back to town.

I need to see Owen. I think Bea does, too.

Her dad heads straight for the emergency vet's office. He actually uses his police siren to get there are quickly as possible. I've never been in a cruiser before, it's fun watching all the cars move over to let us through.

We take Peanut and the two kittens inside to see the vet. The vet sees Peanut, runs over, and takes him quickly into the exam room. He comes out a while later and tells us the Peanut does have a head injury, will need fluids, and has to stay at least overnight. He says it looks like someone hit Peanut with something. He says it didn't appear to be from a fall.

Bea and I look at each other and say, "Vic."
Her dad just nods his head in disgrace.

The vet tells us Peanut will need some stitches, and we can come back tomorrow to pick him up.

The vet then sees the two kittens in our arms.

"And who do we have here?" he asks.

We tell him we found them near the lake and they were all alone. He tells us he wants us to leave them with him. He'll clean them up, give them their shots, and check them over. We can also pick them up tomorrow.

I look at Bea and say, "That works out good. It will give us time to convince our moms that we need to keep the kittens."

Bea says, "Exactly." We start laughing.

Bea's dad drives us home, and we're both exhausted from the day. As we get out of the car, Owen, my parents, Bea's mom, and Bea's papa are all waiting for us. They all rush over and hug us. Owen mouths the word 'sorry.' Of course, he'd go and tell everyone what went down.

We all head to Bea's back deck and finally get to sit and relax. Bea's mom made dinner for everyone, and we talked about what had happened today.

When we finish, both Bea and I tell everyone we're going to bed. I tell Bea that I'm going to go home to sleep in my own bed, and she seems relieved. I'm sure she wants her own bed, too. We hug each other

and tell each other we'll meet up in the morning at
the big rock.

Beatrice

I love Chloe, but I need to get a good night's sleep. I'm so happy she wants to sleep at her house, and I can stay at mine.

After we hug and each turn to leave, I see Owen and go over to talk to him. We walk around the front of the house to have a minute alone. Finally. I thank him for all his help. He tells me he'll always be there for me. As he says that, I think I hope I live long enough for that to be true.

He leans in to give me a hug, and our lips meet. We kiss, and not a small peck on the lips, but a long, sweet kiss. It's perfect.

We pull apart and tell each other we'll talk in the morning. He asks me out on an official date for this weekend. I'm so excited. I can't wait to tell Chloe. Now I just have to figure out what to wear on our date.

Chloe

The rest of the 'Summer of C' is perfect. We spend our days at the beach. School starts in a week, and I'm dreading the summer's end. Bea's doctor still hasn't approved her to go back to school, so at least for the start of school, Bea will do school work from home. I'm in charge of bringing home her schoolwork. It's the least I can do for my best friend.

Mr. McBean is recovering from his injuries. He was beaten up pretty badly at the cabin. He had several broken ribs, a concussion, and one of his lungs collapsed from a gunshot wound. The doctors said it was lucky he was found when he was. He may not have made it otherwise. He came home from the hospital and moved in with Rachel. Rachel smartened up and kicked Kyle out.

Maybe when Bea said life was too short not to have a relationship with her dad, it actually meant something to Rachel. I think coming that close to losing her dad was the wake-up call she needed. She says she wants to get her life in order and work on the relationship between her and her dad. She's trying to stop drinking, smoking, and doing drugs. She looks so much healthier. We go visit Mr. McBean most days. He's so thankful to us for not giving up on him.

Mr. McBean ended up renting the house next to Bea, to a family of five. The Flanders. They moved from a neighborhood on the outskirts of town. I only met the young girl a handful of times and haven't met the older brother yet. Bea said he's in the Army and stationed in Texas. The young girl lives with her parents and the mother's mom. They seem nice. Bea told me the girl Lucy's cute but annoying. She said she talks a lot. That would be annoying.

Lenny made it out of surgery and is back at the service center. He was charged with being an accomplice to the crimes. For now, word is he will probably get probation for his involvement in the crime. Since he was manipulated by Vic and will be testifying against Vic, he probably won't serve any time in prison.

Bea and I agree with this plan. He really isn't a bad egg, and if not for Vic's lies, he'd never have been involved. We went to the shop and visited him once, and he apologized for what he did. He gave us Mr. McBean's lighter to give back to him, too. Mr. McBean cried when we handed it over.

Mr. McBean turned over the missing money to the police after all the court proceedings were done. Apparently, the key to the safe deposit box where the money was located was inside the lighter his wife gave him. Lenny had it the whole time. Seems like a missed opportunity.

Vic will most likely never see the light of day. She's being tried for murder in the first degree, assault and battery with a dangerous weapon, attempted murder, conspiracy to commit murder, and cruelty to animals. Bea's dad said he wouldn't be surprised if they sentenced her to life in prison with no chance of parole.

Peanut is doing great. Mr. McBean gave Peanut to Bea, since he said he wasn't up to taking care of a dog. Turns out, Vic hit Peanut in the head with the handle of her gun. Thankfully, he is healing up fine and almost back to his old self.

Both of our moms let us each keep a kitten. After what we went through, I don't think they had much choice. I named mine Sherlock, and Bea named hers Watson. We picked the names before we found out our male kittens were actually females, but the names stuck, so there you have it.

Owen and Bea have been spending a lot of time together. It was slightly awkward for me to hang with the two of them. Until my brother invited his work friend, Brad, over. Brad is dreamy. We hit it off immediately. I've never been so happy.

The 'Summer of C' was a success.

Until it wasn't.

Beatrice

The 'Summer of C' was truly glorious, even with all the drama around Mr. McBean. It brought me and Chloe even closer, if that was even possible. Everything was going perfectly. I was feeling so much better after starting the injections. The last scan I had showed the cancer tumors shrinking. I have a real chance of beating this cancer.

Owen and I are doing great. Now, with Chloe dating Brad, we spend a lot of time all together. I have a great relationship with my Papa. We spend a lot of time together. I am so thankful he is in my life.

Tommy is still with Angela. I think they deserve each other. I still get mad when I see him hanging around like nothing happened. I hope karma gets back at him someday.

Vic is behind bars waiting for her day in court.

Mr. McBean is on the mend, Peanut is getting back to normal, and he's slowly taking a liking to the kittens. Slowly being the operative word.

I have new neighbors that are renting Mr. McBean's house. They seem nice except the little girl talks endlessly. It's a good thing she is adorable. Things couldn't be going any better.

Until they weren't.

Two days before school started, I was sitting on my back deck with Owen. We were hanging around and waiting for Chloe and Brad to come by. Chloe was home getting ready and Brad was going to go get her and meet at my house.

We were all going to spend the day at the beach. Chloe and I had new bikinis to show off. It was an absolutely beautiful day.

Brad walks onto the deck and asks where Chloe is. I tell him she is supposed to be home getting ready. I reminded him he was supposed to be meeting her there. He says he went to her door, and she didn't answer. That's strange. Where could she be? I just talked to her on the phone this morning. I get up, head over to Chloe's, and knock on the door. Brad is right. She doesn't answer.

I open the door and pop inside. Maybe she's drying her hair and can't hear the doorbell. I search the house but don't find Chloe. I find a note on the kitchen counter that explains where she is. It's a note to her mom telling her she's heading for the beach. It says that Brad, Bea, and Owen are meeting her there.

I'm sure I told her to meet us at my house. Oh well, she probably was too busy being in love with Brad to actually hear me talk to her.

I walk back to my house, grab the guys, and we head down to the beach.

The beach is pretty busy since it's an amazing day today. We put our towels down and look out for Chloe. We don't see her.

We walk along the whole beach and still can't seem to find Chloe. That's strange. The note Chloe left for her mom says she was meeting us at the beach, but she's nowhere to be found.

Brad looks concerned. He says he talked to her on the phone last night and everything was fine.

I say, "Brad, did she say anything weird? Did it seem like anything was bothering her?"

Brad says, "I'm not exactly sure. She seemed a little distracted. I figured she was just tired."

"Did you ask her if anything was bothering her?"

Brad responds, "I asked her, but she said she was tired and not to worry. It was strange, now that I think back, about how she said goodbye."

"What do you mean? Strange? What did she say? I ask.

"Usually, we just say goodnight and that we'll talk in the morning. She said she had a bad feeling something was going to happen. She said she was happy we met. She said she was happy being with me. Then, she told me to take care and to promise me always to be there for you and Owen. It was weird, but I thought she was just being emotional. I told her she would feel better after a good night's sleep. She said that I was right, that it was probably nothing, and we hung up."

"That is weird. I wonder what she thought was going to happen. Where could she be?"

"Hey, look at this." Owen is pointing down at the sand. I look over and see a book. It looks like the book Chloe was reading. Maybe it wasn't hers. I pick it up and open it up. It is Chloe's. The bookmark I gave her is inside. Why would she leave it?

We talk about the book and decide we need to find my dad. Now.

Chloe

I don't know why I was so distracted last night talking to Brad. I kept having the feeling that something bad was going to happen. I felt the same way before I learned about Bea's cancer diagnosis. It's not a good feeling at all.

I woke up this morning with the same feeling. I really thought it would be gone after a good night's sleep. I jump in the shower and grab my stuff for the beach.

On my way out, I leave a note for my mom. I am pretty sure Brad said to meet him at the beach. I grab my bag and head to the beach. I love my new bikini and can't wait for Brad to see it. The beach is probably going to be packed since it's such a beautiful day.

Beatrice

It's been four hours since anyone has seen or heard from Chloe. Where is she? She wouldn't have left without telling anyone.

My parents, Chloe's parents, and I are all sitting in Chloe's house, waiting. Waiting for what we don't know. My dad has patrols searching the town. Some are in the Hemlock Lake area. Brad and Owen are still walking around the beach, trying to find her. She simply vanished. This can't be happening. Where is she?

I heard my parents ask her parents if they thought she would run away. That is beyond crazy talk. She never would've left on her own. I know she wouldn't leave me. Not in a million years. We're best friends. We had our future planned.

Please, God, please find Chloe. Bring her home. If you have to take someone, then take me and spare her. I was supposed to be the one gone, not Chloe. Please bring her back. Please, God, please.

She has to come back. Chloe, I need you.

Chloe

My eyes are heavy. My head hurts. What happened? Where am I? Did I get hit by a car? I remember walking to the beach, then darkness. I am having a hard time seeing. It's so dark. I don't know where I am. I am sitting on a cement, cold floor. My eyes are slowly adjusting to the dark.

I have no idea where I am. It looks like a closet or a super small room. Maybe a basement? There is a super small window with a little light shining thru. It's still daytime. I left the house early. I try to move my hand to my head. My head hurts so much.

My arm won't move. It's stuck to the floor. Wait, it's chained to the floor. I can hear the rattle when I try to move my hand. I am in full-fledged panic mode. I can't move. It's so dark. Where am I?

I scream. I am crying, screaming. No one is coming. Please, God, help me. I hear what seems to be a doorknob turning. Is someone coming in? I scream for help. Please help me, I scream over and over.

The door opens. Thank god someone is coming to save me. There's a light behind the door. I can see someone standing in the doorway. I can't make out who it is. Not yet. The person moves out of the shadow, and I can almost see who it is.

Mr. McBean?

"Thank God you're here. How did you find me? I have never been so happy to see you than now. You are my hero. Where am I? I am so happy you found me. Did you find a key to the chains? I want to go home. Why are you just standing there? Help me? What are you doing?"

The door slams shut. I don't understand. Why did you close the door? Aren't you here to save me? Then I hear my premonition in my head, "You will never leave here alive."

Marshmallow.

I scream until I can't scream anymore.

Darkness overtakes me.

Beatrice

All we can do is wait. My dad and his deputies are talking to everyone in town. It seems like she just vanished. No one has seen or heard anything. How's that even possible? In a town this small, you would think someone would have seen something.

I know, in my heart, she didn't run away. The local papers keep saying that she may have, but they don't know Chloe like I do. I also heard people say she walked into the ocean and killed herself. I know that can't be true since, like me, she hated the ocean. She would never run away or kill herself. She's out there, and I need to find her.

The next week is a blur. Chloe is gone, and I feel dead inside.

I stop over to see Chloe's mom. She asks me if I will hold on to something for her, from Chloe, until she comes home. I say, of course, anything. I want nothing more than to believe Chloe will come back home. She leaves the room and comes back with Sherlock. She tells me that Chloe would want the kittens together, just as she would've wanted to stay together with me. I am crying and through the tears, I take Sherlock and head for home. Home where life will never be the same until Chloe comes home.

I had no idea the 'Summer of C' would mean the 'Summer of Chloe'.

Beatrice

My dad walked into my room and put the light on. I was just sitting in the dark, thinking about Chloe. I wish I knew what happened. Where could she be? It just makes no sense.

"What's up, Dad? Is everything okay? Did you find Chloe?"

"Bea. It's about Chloe. I know you've heard all the rumors that people are spreading. I've heard the same ones. Some say she ran away from home, others say she probably killed herself in the ocean, and I even heard someone say a UFO took her. We both know that none of those are true."

"Dad, I know she's out there somewhere."

"I need to tell you there has been a development in the investigation. I want you to hear it from me first. Chloe's parents received a call asking for a ransom in order to have Chloe come home."

"What? Are you serious? Who called them? Someone has here?"

"Bea, let me finish. I know this is upsetting. The call came this morning. We are not even sure it is legit at this time. Could be someone just trying to take advantage of her parents? We have no proof of anything yet. I need to head to the station and see what I can find out. I will get in touch with you as soon as I know anything. I promise.

"Bea, we will not stop looking until we find her, I promise."

"Dad, I am scared."

"I know, I know." My dad leans over and hugs me.

"Thanks, Dad. I love you."

He leans down, kisses my forehead, and says, "Love you more."

Beatrice

Each day that passes is endless. I miss Chloe.

I am sitting on my deck, thinking about Chloe, when I hear someone yelling.

I jumped up to see what was going on.

My mom is standing at the mailbox, shaking. I run over to see what scared her. That's when I see it.

A note in her hands. I take it from her and read it. It says,

> *Money for Chloe. Next is Bea.*

Chloe is alive. Now I just need to find her. I will find her or die trying.

I collapse to the ground.

Lucy

I hear the sirens before I see them pull up to the house next door. The ambulance parks in front of my new best friend's house. I wonder if everything is ok. Maybe Bea's dad is sick. Bea is my best friend. I go see her all the time. I think she likes it when I talk a lot. My nana says I talk too much, but I don't think that is a thing. I am almost seven years old and I have a lot to say.

When I first met Bea, she said her name was Beatrice, but her friends call her Bea. She told me I could call her Bea. That's how I knew she wanted to be my best friend. She wouldn't have asked me to call her Bea if we weren't supposed to be best friends. She is so nice and easy to talk to.

I peek out the window and see some guys in blue outfits leaning over someone on the ground. I can't tell who it is. I better run out and see who it is. It's probably her dad. He's old.

Beatrice

I can hear people talking. I can't see anything. I try to talk, but no words come out. I think I am on the ground. It's hard. I can hear my mom sobbing. She keeps asking someone if I am ok. Am I not ok? I don't know what's going on. I remember running over to the mailbox. I just remembered the note. CHLOE. Who has her? Where is she? Please be ok Chloe. Why would someone want me? I feel some people touching me. Something is squeezing my arm. I hear someone say that my blood pressure is low. I feel someone put some tube of air in my nose. What is happening? Something stabs me in my hand. I know that feeling. It must be an IV line. I have had enough of those with my cancer to know what that feels like. I still can't open my eyes. This feels like a nightmare.

I hear my mom tell someone to go home. It takes me a minute to realize she is talking to Lucy. Lucy must have seen the ambulance come. Poor Lucy. She is probably scared.

I feel like I am being lifted. I am being lifted. I am now on something softer, a bed? Then I hear what no one wants to hear about themselves, "we are going to transfer your daughter to County Medical. You should meet us there. She is in a bad way."

Chloe

My body hurts. Where am I?

Then, I remember. I am trapped. Fear washes over me. I thought I saw Mr. McBean. Was it him? No. it wasn't him. I am sure it was someone else, but who?

Who would keep me here? This doesn't make any sense.

I scream, "HELP ME, SOMEONE HELP ME!"

No one responds.

Then I hear the door opening. I am trying to adjust my eyes to see who it is. There is a woman in the doorway. She is carrying a tray of what looks like food. She puts it on a small table next to me. I yell, "Who are you? What are you doing? Let me go!"

She sits on a stool across from me and finally starts talking.

"Morning Chloe. I know you are wondering why you are here. I won't hurt you if you behave. You need to be quiet here, no screaming. You can get up and walk around some. You are chained to the floor, but you have enough chains to walk around and use the bathroom. I will bring you food a few times a day. I need you to be quiet and not yell anymore. I don't want to hurt you or drug you again. You won't be here long if everything goes as planned."

"What is your plan? I want to go home? Who are you? What do you want with me? I don't even know who you are."

"Chloe, Chloe, Chloe. That is a lot of questions. You do not need to worry yourself about my plans yet. Just behave and no one will get hurt. Because of you and your friend Beatrice, something very dear to me is gone. Someone has to pay for that. I don't want to hurt you. Your parents need to pay for what you did. Same for Beatrice. I need to get your little friend Beatrice to join us before I can explain any more. For you to make it home in one piece, hinges on Beatrice and your families. Now, eat your dinner, and get comfortable. Next thing you know, your other half will be here with you, and we can finish this. I've brought you a few books to read to give you something to do. No need to thank me."

She laughs as she heads out the door. I hear the door being locked, and it is quiet again.

I cry. She looks familiar. I know I have seen her before. But where?

Lucy

I hear voices. Someone is talking. I don't know who it is. It sounds muffled. Who is it? I can't see anyone, just hear someone talking. That's strange. If I had more time, I would try to see who it is, but I need to see who is outside on the ground.

I run outside and can't believe what I see. On the ground, I see Bea. Two guys are around her with needles, a tube, and a black thing around her arm. I hear them talking to Bea's mom. They say they are taking my bestie to the hospital. What happened?

I run over to Bea's mom to find out. She is crying. She tells me to go home. I want to stay with Bea. She tells me again to go home.

I run home to find my mom.

I run into my house, and my mom sees me and knows something is wrong. I tell her what I saw. I tell her about Bea. I can't catch my breath.

My mom sits me down and tells me everything will be alright. I don't know how she knows this, but it makes me feel better. She's usually always right. She gets me a drink and a snack. She sits with me until I feel better. We hear the ambulance drive past the house and I know Bea is inside. She has to be alright, she just has to.

My mom tells me we are going to walk to the beach with my nana to meet my little brother. She packs up lunch and we head out. She tells me she will call Bea's mom later to see how she is. That makes me feel better too.

We easily find my brother at the beach. It is warm and sunny. We lay out our blanket and have our lunch. My mom tells my nana about Bea. She seems upset about Bea too. She kept saying, "That's a pickle, isn't it?"

Not exactly sure what pickles have to do with Bea at the hospital? Maybe they give sick people pickles? I hope I never get sick. I hate pickles.

Beatrice

I must have fallen deeper to sleep. It takes me a few minutes to remember where I am. I think I am at the hospital. I still can't open my eyes or talk. I can only hear things going on around me. I hear my mom talking to my dad. My dad is here? I didn't know he was here now. My mom asks what is taking so long? I am not sure what she is talking about. My dad tells her the doctor will be in shortly. He tells her to try to relax. He says that she is in the right place. It takes a second to realize they are talking about me. I try to talk, but nothing comes out.

I hear my mom say the word 'finally'. Someone else is in the room. I can only listen.

"Mr. and Mrs. Chase, my name is Dr. Kennedy. I am the attending physician today. I am here to update you on your daughter's condition and to tell you we will admit her to the ICU. Right now, her vitals are within normal limits, her blood work is still pending, she is stable. But there certainly is brain swelling that we are concerned about. We have talked to her oncologist, Dr. Skinner. She is on her way. We are not sure if her condition is because of her cancer progression, or a secondary infection. The stress she is under with her friend could be exacerbating her condition. Her oncologist will be able to conclusively determine what has happened. We are giving her steroids to help with

the brain inflammation, fluids for hydration, and pain medication for any of her discomfort. As of right now, she is in a sleep state. She cannot communicate, but we believe she can hear you. I would suggest you talk to her and reassure her she is in excellent hands. We will continue to monitor her and wait for Dr. Skinner to arrive. Do you have any questions?"

My mom is crying. My dad says he doesn't have any follow-up questions.

I hear the door open and close. I assume the doctor left. I can hear my mom and dad in the room. They are both crying.

Then sleep overtakes me.

I dream of Chloe. We are sitting on the dock, overlooking Hemlock Lake. It is a beautiful day, the weather is warm, the water still, and I feel at peace.

Lucy

My brother is out in the water. He is hanging with some kids he met the other day at the beach. My mom and Nana are talking about Bea. I need to get away. I tell my mom I am going to look for some seashells. I tell her I am going to get them for Bea. She tells me to be careful. I grab my bucket and head down closer to the water.

The water is warm. I like putting my feet in. It's fun when the water rushes up and tickles my toes. Unless I feel seaweed, then it's not too fun.

I start to search for pretty seashells. I find a few right away and put them in my bucket. Bea will love them. After I find about twenty more to add to my bucket, I see something shiny partially buried in the sand. I get close to it so I can see what it is. It's a bracelet. It's covered in sand, so I rinse it in the water. It's pretty. It's green and has a charm with the letter B on it. Maybe the B is for best friend, or for Bea. Either way, it's mine now. Finders keepers. I put it on. It fits perfectly. It's beautiful. I never had a pretty bracelet before. I love it. I grab my shells and run to show my mom. We talk about how pretty it is as we head back home.

Chloe

This can't be happening. Who is the old lady and what could she possibly want with me and Bea? I need to get out of here. I look around but see no way out. The only light is from a tiny window. It is too far for me to reach it with the chain on my wrist. I work to pull off the chain, but it is too tight. That's when I realized my bracelet was missing. I search around me but it's not there. How could I have lost it? I have worn it for years. Maybe the old crazy lady took it. The missing bracelet seems like the least of my problems, but it makes me sad. I need to find a way out.

I can't help but talk out loud and ask for help. I am not even talking to anyone, since I know no one is listening, but it is too quiet here.

"Can anyone hear me? Help me? Can someone please help me? Marshmallow. I just want Bea."

Silence comes back to me.

Lucy

We walk back from the beach and I go right in the house and rinse off my beautiful shells. Bea is going to love them. My mom said she would call to see how Bea was doing later on. I hope my bestie is ok. I want to show her my new bracelet and give her all her new shells.

My mom sends me to my room to change out of my bathing suit. I think that is stupid since it's only a little wet. She's talking to my nana, so I don't fight it and head to my room. I think I'll just put on shorts and a t-shirt over it. Taking it off seems dumb. She won't even be able to tell.

I sit on the floor and look for my favorite T-shirt in the bottom drawer of my bureau. It's blue and has a unicorn on the front. Then I hear it. A voice. Someone is talking. I can't see anyone. The voice is coming from my closet.

I can hear someone say that they are scared and don't know where they are.

I think I know who it is.

I think I have a ghost.

My friend Rosie from school told me she has one in her house. I didn't believe her, but now I think I have one too. She thought she was so special that she had one. Wait till I tell her I have one. What else could it be?

I have been asking God to send me one too so I could be like Rosie. He finally sent me one. I knew if I was good, he would send one. I better change out of my bathing suit. I don't want him to get mad and take my ghost away. I wanted one so bad. Yippee. I have one too. I can still hear the voice, but don't see anyone.

Finally, I have my very own ghost. In your face, stupid Rosie.

Beatrice

It comes back to me where I am. I am still in the hospital. It smells like cleaner. I hear someone talking. It's my mom. I can hear her talking to someone. It sounds like Dr. Skinner. I try to talk so that they know I am alive, but no words come out. I feel trapped. I can't see or speak. It's like I am dead.

I hear Dr. Skinner tell my mom that she is uncertain what is causing my condition. She says that I am non-responsive. That sounds horrifying. My mom asks when I will wake up. I want to yell that I am right here. I am alive. But no words come out. Dr. Skinner says only time will tell. She says the first thing they need to do is get the brain swelling down. Then I heard her say, "It is time for prayers. It is possible that the cancer has progressed faster than expected and she may not recover. You, as a family, may have some decisions to make to help her find peace."

My mom is crying uncontrollably. Then I hear Dr. Skinner tell her she will leave her be and will check back shortly.

Is it possible that I will die? That I won't wake up. This is not what I thought would happen. I didn't even get to say goodbye to anyone. I didn't tell Chloe how important she was to me. It was supposed to be besties for the resties. I didn't think resties meant this soon. I didn't give Owen a kiss goodbye. My parents? I didn't say goodbye. It can't end like this. I know I am supposed to die, but I need more time. I am not ready to go. Please, God. Please give me more time. Please.

Chloe

There is no way out. I have been trying and trying to get free. I have yelled 'help me' until my throat hurts. There is no way out. No one to talk to. No one to listen. This is a nightmare. I need to get free. Please, God. Please.

Then I hear the doorknob turn. The old lady is back. She is carrying another tray of food. I ate the last tray of food, it wasn't too good, but I thought I needed to keep my strength up if I had a chance to run. I need to find a way out. I try to lose myself in the book the old lady brought, but it is hard to concentrate.

"You are awake. Nice to see you are reading your book. I wasn't sure what book you would want. I picked this one since my daughter had to read it when she was young. I have some bad news."

"I don't care about your news. I want to get out of here. Let me go. I want to go home."

"Sorry, Chloe. Can't let you go yet. We have a situation with your friend Beatrice. She got herself in a bit of trouble. Seems like an ambulance had to scrape her off the ground after she passed out. She is in the hospital as we speak. Wonder if she will make it?"

"Stop! You're lying. Stop saying something bad happened to Bea. You don't know anything. You're just trying to scare me."

"I wish I was lying. It makes the situation much more difficult. What should have been a simple thing to bring Bea here and get your parents to give us the ransom now has to change. You better hope she lives and we can bring her here. Someone has to pay."

"Who are you?"

"I'll give you a hint. Mike."

"Mike? Mike, the guy that Vic shot? What does that have to do with you? Or me and Bea? We didn't shoot him."

"It has a lot to do with all of us. That is enough talking for now. Relax and pray your little friend makes it."

All I could do was cry.

The old lady walked out and locked the door. One of these times, maybe she will forget to lock the door behind her. Fingers crossed.

Lucy

I spend a lot of time in my room lately since it seems like that is where my ghost friend talks to me the most. I don't think anyone else has heard my ghost. No one has mentioned her. I don't want to say anything either, in case it freaks someone out and they make her leave. I have tried talking to the ghost, but she can't hear me. I named her Boo. I like it sounds like a scary word, but I ain't scared. She only asks for help to get her back home. I think she is probably stuck here after dying and can't find heaven. I think heaven is up in the clouds. Maybe the ceiling is stopping her. I keep leaving my window open to see if that helps, but so far it hasn't worked.

Boo must be resting, since she hasn't talked in a little while.

I walk in the kitchen to see if mom has any snacks out. She is sitting at the table with Nana talking.

"Hi there, honey. What are you up to in your room?"

"Nothing, just playing with my dollhouse. Can I have a snack?"

"Of course. How about some pretzels?"

"Yummy. Thanks, Momma."

"Lucy, me and Nana were talking about Beatrice. We think it might be nice if we bring you to visit her. Her dad said it would be ok for you to see her. What do you think?"

"YES!" I yell louder than I thought. I'm so excited. I can't wait to see Bea and give her the shells. She probably has been so sad that I haven't been able to talk to her. She's probably begging her dad to see me. "Can we go now?"

"Sure honey. Go get ready. We'll leave soon."

I leave my snack and run toward my room. As I leave the kitchen, I hear my nana say to my mom, "Bringing Lucy to see Beatrice is a brilliant idea. It's the only way we can see how she is and see how we can get her here."

Beatrice

I have no idea how long I have been here. I know a lot of different doctors and nurses have come and gone. I haven't been able to talk. No one knows if I will be ok. I hear the doctors talk to my mom and dad and say the words 'only time will tell', 'pray', and 'she needs to fight'. How do I fight when I can't even move?

My mom has been at my bedside the whole time. Every time I am aware of where I am, she is there with me. I don't think I told her I love her enough. I want another chance to tell her I love her and that I am sorry I yelled at her. I don't want her not to know how much she means to me.

I have had a few visitors come in. My papa came in a few times and sat near the bed. He held my hand and told me some stories about my grandma. You can tell by his stories how much he loved her. He told me he was so glad he was able to meet me. He told me I remind him of my grandma. I can hear him crying.

Owen comes in to see me a lot. He sits next to me and holds my hand. He doesn't seem to know what to say. I think he cries sometimes but tries to hide it. I can hear him take his glasses off to dry his eyes. When he talks, he talks about places and things we can do together when I get better. I hope I get better. All the things he says sound like fun.

Lucy comes in to see me, too. Sometimes too much. She is the only visitor that I wish wouldn't talk so much. She gives me a headache. I want to wake up just to stop her from talking. She tells me about each shell she has found. Each Individual shell. It felt like she talked forever. She tells me she has a secret and that I can't tell anyone. Umm, Lucy, I can't talk. She tells me she has a ghost in her house. She rambles on and on about her ghost and how Rosie, her friend, isn't so smug anymore about her ghost. I need to wake up so I can tell her to shut up. She is a great kid, but man alive, stop talking.

Chloe

I am so worried about what the old lady said about Bea. Is it true Bea is at the hospital? Is it her cancer? I can't stop thinking about Bea. She can't die without knowing I'm alright. She can't die without saying goodbye. I need to get out of here and get to Bea.

The old lady came back, dropped the tray, and left. She wouldn't tell me anything about Bea or her connection to Mike. I begged, and she told me to be quiet and walked out. And, of course, she locked the door behind her.

I keep trying to get the chain off my wrist. I take the fork off the tray each time she comes and try to pry it open. It seems to get looser. Maybe it is only wishful thinking.

To waste time and fight the quiet, I read the book out loud. The book is actually on my reading list for school, coincidentally. Bea is supposed to read it too. I wonder if she is reading it too. Knowing that makes me feel good, like we still have a connection. The book is <u>Of Mice and Men</u>. It's about two friends and their summer adventure. Of course, their adventure has a lot of animals getting killed and Bea's and mine didn't.

I read out loud. I am at the part where Lennie gets a puppy. George seems happy for Lennie.

Beatrice

I am losing hope. Each day seems like a lifetime. I am in a nightmare. Caught between the conscious world and moving on to the next. My mind is clear. I can hear, think, and remember, but my body is lost. I can't move at all, can't open my eyes, and can't talk. If my life is going to be like this forever, then I am ready to die. This is not living.

Then I hear her. Lucy is back. Great. As I think that I am rolling my eyes. Of course, no one can see me doing it.

Lucy is rambling on about her ghost. Does she really believe she has a ghost? I'm not convinced there is such a thing as a ghost. I kind of hope so. That way, when I die, I'll be able to visit my family and Chloe. I probably would only watch what everyone was up to just to see what I was missing. That seems sad. Maybe I don't want to be a ghost.

Lucy's ghost seems to want to find her way home, so maybe she doesn't want to be a ghost either.

Lucy tells me a story about someone named George and Lennie. I don't know a George and I don't think she's talking about the Lenny I know. She's saying something about the two guys on an adventure in California. Now she's saying something about Lennie getting a new puppy. The story sounds familiar but I can't place it. I

"

think I have heard it before. Maybe it's a story that I heard when I was younger. I'm not sure, but I feel like I know it.

I hear some other people come into the room. Lucy calls one Momma and the other Nana. I only met her mom once before. She was nice enough. I never met her nana.

I hear someone say, "She looks bad. That won't be good if she dies. No one is going to give us any money for a dead girl. We will have to pressure the other one's family for more, I guess."

Who said that? Maybe I am not as clear as I thought I was. Maybe I misunderstood what they said. Why would anyone want me to die? And who else do they want dead? I must be confused. That makes no sense.

Then I feel someone hold my hand. Owen is back. All feels right.

Chloe

It seems like all I do is read out loud. Lennie ended up killing the puppy. That was sad. I thought Lennie was a gentle giant. Now I think he isn't too gentle. Now Lennie is upset about killing the puppy. Curly's wife is trying to comfort him. That's sweet. He's stroking her hair, he's calming down. Super sweet. Oh no, Lennie just snapped her neck. Now she's dead too. Lennie clearly was not so gentle.

The chain around my wrist finally comes off. I still have no way to get out, but at least the chain is off. When I hear the old lady come in, I put it back on so she won't know. One of these times, I am going to rush her and try to break free. She just has to get close enough to me. I will only have one chance. I am sure I can push her down. She doesn't look that strong.

For now, I need to be patient.

Beatrice

I am so glad my mom is with me all the time. Having her next to me gives me comfort. I heard the doctor tell her that the latest brain scan has shown some improvement. The doctor said the medication was relieving the pressure in my brain. The doctor said I was not out of the woods, but she was cautiously optimistic. I didn't even know I was in the woods.

Lucy's back. I can't wait to get better so I can have a Lucy break. Ugh.

She's back to her story of George and Lennie. Lennie just killed the puppy. What kind of story is this? Did she make it up? Who would make up a story like this? Now she's saying someone's wife, Curly's wife, is trying to calm Lennie down. Wait, what did she just say? Lennie snapped her neck. What? What kind of story is this?

I have heard this story before. Wait. I have read this story before. I think it's the book I have from school. She is too young to read it. Who would read it to her? I need to think clearly. I can feel I am so close to something, I just can't seem to get there. What am I missing?

Lucy

I love sitting with Bea. I have been telling her all sorts of stories. I am sure she loves me talking to her. I have been telling her the story of George and Lennie. My ghost has been telling me the story and then I come and see Bea and tell her. I told Bea that I made up the story even though I didn't. That way, Bea will think that I am super smart. I figure since she's sleeping, she won't know the difference.

My mom and Nana come to see Bea with me sometimes. I'm not sure why. They seem super interested if Bea will get better or not. I even heard them ask the nurses a few times, but the nurses won't say. I've heard them talk about Chloe too, but don't understand what for. I don't think Chloe is a very good friend to Bea, since I haven't seen her visit once.

I'm sitting next to Bea, telling her more of my story. Since we are besties, I can tell she likes me talking. We have the connection only besties can have. I hold her hand so she knows I miss her. I wish she would wake up. Please Bea, wake up.

And then I feel it. She squeezes my hand. Bestie squeezed my hand. I scream.

Beatrice

I hear Lucy scream. I scream. Then it hits me. I can scream. I can talk. My vision is cloudy, but I am starting to see. It's becoming clearer.

My mom and dad come rushing in. They looked stunned. I can't believe it either. I am awake. They yell for the nurse. A young nurse comes in and says she will get the doctor.

Everyone is talking at once. My mom is asking me if I am ok. My dad is asking me if I know where I am. Lucy's trying to tell me about George and Lennie. I don't know who to focus on. It is all too much. I yell for everyone to stop talking. I need a minute.

Dr. Skinner rushes into the room. She also looks stunned but happy. She's smiling. She tells everyone to step out so she can examine me. After everyone leaves, she explains what happened to me. She tells me how I collapsed, how I had swelling in my brain, how I was kept medicated to give my body time to recoup.

I ask if I could see my mom.

Dr. Skinner gets up to go and turns and says, "I am glad you're back, Bea." and she leaves.

My mom comes in alone. She comes over to my bed and I start to cry. Then she starts to cry. I tell her how sorry I am that I yelled at her and that I love her so much. She tells me she is so proud of me and that she never doubted that I loved her. She apologized for not being there for me. I tell her I know she was with me when it mattered most. We hug. I feel at peace.

Beatrice

The next few days are full of tests and physical therapy to get my strength back. I have had a lot of visitors too. My papa, Owen, and Chloe's parents stopped by. Even Mr. McBean came by to see how I was doing. And of course, Lucy.

Chloe still is missing. Her family is still waiting to hear more about the ransom.

Lucy continued to talk about her ghost friend. She really believes she has a ghost. Clearly, they are best friends too. She continues with her George and Lennie's story. I have figured out it was the book I was supposed to read for school. She still says she made it up. I don't say anything since with her telling me the story, I won't have to read it again.

She gets up to leave and grabs my hand to say she is happy I am alive and not another ghost. That's when I see it.

Her bracelet.

"Lucy, where did you get that bracelet?"

"It's mine. It has the letter B on it. The B means bestie."

"Lucy. I think the bracelet is Chloe's. See, I have one too." I pull my hand out from under the blankets and show her.

Lucy looks at and shakes her head. "Nope, this is mine. Yours is different. Yours has a C on it, not a B. Besides, a lot of people have bracelets. My ghost even talks about her bracelet. She has the same one as me."

"What do you mean? Your ghost has one too? How do you know your ghost has one too?"

"She talks about it. She keeps looking for hers. She probably can't see it. But it sounds like mine. I know a lot about my ghost. I know her favorite snack since she tells me that a lot. She has a brother like me, too."

"What is her favorite food, Lucy?"

"Marshmallows."

I yell out, "Someone get my dad! I need to see my dad."

Beatrice

After what seems like an eternity, my dad comes into my room.

I am crying.

He runs over and I finally get the words out, "Dad, I know where Chloe is!"

Chloe

The days seem to never end. Each day is like the last. Old lady comes in, drops food and leaves. She won't answer my questions. I keep trying to get out, but it seems like an impossibility. Then things change.

The old lady came in with her tray of food and told me the worst thing. She tells me that Bea is dead. I cry uncontrollably. She told me she passed away, and that I was next. She tells me they have no choice but to kill me. She says that I know too much and my parents haven't come up with the money yet. She says that once I am gone, they will finally be able to put the past behind them and move on with their life.

I am crying and cannot stop. Bea cannot be gone. I don't want to be without her. It was supposed to be besties for the resties.

The old lady tells me to shut up and leaves.

Then a miracle happens.

She forgets to lock the door behind her.

Lucy

Who does Bea think she is? I know the bracelet is mine and I'm not giving it up. She should be happy that I have a bracelet that matches hers. I thought she was my best friend, but maybe she isn't after all. My ghost hasn't asked for the bracelet back. Ghosts can see everything. She would have seen it on me and never said she wanted mine. Maybe she is my best friend and not Bea. I should take my shells back from Bea and see how she likes that.

I hear my Nana yell, "STOP!" from outside my bedroom window.

Chloe

I quietly turn the doorknob and peek out the door. I don't see anyone. I run. I run outside and bolt down the street. I hear the old lady yelling at me to stop. I run faster. I look back and she is running after to me. She can't keep up. Someone is running with her, she is faster. She is gaining on me. I have no energy. Adrenaline keeps me going.

Someone grabs me.

It isn't the old lady or her friend.

It's Bea's dad.

I am safe. I collapse in his arms.

I cry and say "Bea."

Her dad hugs me and says Bea is going to be alright. He tells me he will take me to her. Bea isn't dead. She is alive. I need to get to Bea.

I look back and see the old lady and Lucy's mom being handcuffed.

Then I only look ahead.

Beatrice

The door to the hospital room opens and I see my dad walk in. Right behind him is Chloe. We are both crying hysterically. Through the tears, we both say, "Marshmallow."

Beatrice

I am so happy that Chloe has been found. I cannot even image life without her. She means everything to me.

The doctors checked her out and all in all she was in good shape. No need to be admitted to the hospital. Since I was still not out of the woods, my dad did his cop stuff interviews in my room. Chloe and my dad sat near my hospital bed going over the details of her kidnapping. Chloe told us that the old lady, who now we know was Mike's widow, pulled her car next to Chloe when she was walking to the beach. She told Chloe that Peanut was really sick and needed her help. Chloe remembers saying she had to run home and the next she knew she woke up locked in a basement.

We talked about how she would talk to herself because she was scared and lonely. She talked about how she read the <u>Of Mice and Men</u> school book out loud to make the time go by. She said she never saw anyone else other than the old lady. She didn't know she was being held in McBean's house.

Her parents rushed into my hospital room and couldn't stop crying. They had been working endlessly to try to get the ransom money together. They figure now, that since I was in the hospital, the plan to get the ransom was put on hold. Just as well, since they were having a hard time coming up with the cash.

After the interview was over I asked my dad if they could bring Lucy in.

Lucy was waiting outside and came in a few minutes later. She was crying. I think she was confused about everything that went down. She had no idea her ghost was actually Chloe. She said she felt bad not knowing. Me and Chloe sat with her and made sure she knew how she saved the day. I would not have put together that Lucy's ghost was Chloe without hearing the word marshmallow. I told Lucy that I was proud of her. We joked about how something good actually came out of her talking too much. No matter what happens I know we will always be friends.

Dr. Skinner discharged me from the hospital a few days later. I still was not able to go back to school, but the doctor thought me being admitted to the hospital was not from my cancer diagnosis. She thinks my issues were from collapsing to the ground after hearing Chloe was being held for ransom. Chloe and I quickly healed from our emotional and physical issues. We do think even with all that went down, the 'Summer of C' was a success. So much so that we reinvented of 'Summer of C', to the 'Fall of Fun'. With FUN being the optimal word.

One other thing you should know, is both Chloe and I aced our <u>Of Mice and Men</u> book reports. Thanks to Lucy and her big, beautiful mouth.

One Year Later

I am cancer-free. The last scan confirms I am in remission. I will continue to see Dr. Skinner for scans and blood work, but she is thrilled with my results. I feel alive.

Owen and I are going strong. We are spending all of our time together. Brad and Chloe ended up breaking up right after she came home. He said he didn't know what was going to happen to her and wanted to date other people. Chloe ended up dating Stu, of all people. He is great, and she seems so happy. We all spend a lot of time together too, so we all are best friends. We all are talking about college and want to all go to school together. I want to go to school for criminal justice. Owen wants to be a pharmacist, Stu wants to go to college for business management, and Chloe wants to be a zookeeper. We joke about her only wanting that profession because she was trapped like an animal. It's funny now, not so much a year ago.

Lucy's mom and Nana are in jail waiting for trial. The old lady ended up being Mr. McBean's friend, Mike's widow. She and her daughter set the whole kidnapping up to get retaliation for Mike getting killed by Vic. Apparently, they blamed me and Chloe for stirring the pot with trying to find Mr. McBean. They figured Mike would still be alive if we didn't start our search. They wanted money so they could move away and start over.

Lucy moved out to live with her dad. Someone gave her our phone number, so she calls, a lot, to talk. Yay, me. In her eyes, we're still besties. I keep praying a real ghost moves in with her and she can have a new bestie, but so far, she only has me.

My relationship with my mom couldn't be any better. We are in a good place with each other and I am proud to call her my mom.

My dad and mom are doing great too. They act like they are reliving their honeymoon period. It creeps me out, but I am happy for them.

Chloe has and will always be my best friend. I never want to imagine life without her. We will always be each other's besties for the resties.

Acknowledgements

I am fortunate to have several people in my life who I can rely and depend on. Without your love and friendship I would not be who I am today. I would like to thank each of you for your loving support.

My husband, Alan, who is my best friend. I cannot imagine living my best life with anyone else by my side. Love you always. Kisses.

My son, Matt, who I certainly could not have completed this book without his tech support. I love you so much and am proud of the young man you are. Continue to save all the lives.

My daughter, Emily, who has re-read my book draft way too many times without hesitation. Thank you for being my reading buddy. You are beyond beautiful. I love you more.

My extended family, who has patiently been listening to the book status for so long I am surprised they still want me around. John, Tim, and Cathy, I am so thankful we have become closer. Love you.

My bestie for being my bestie for the restie, always.

My BFry for sharing my DNA. Laughing with you means more than you can ever realize. My life has become so much better with you in it. Thank you to my mom for bringing us together.

www.ingramcontent.com/pod-product-compliance
Lightning Source LLC
Chambersburg PA
CBHW022012310726
48972CB00006B/1622